OCEAN BLISS & GRISLY BITS

A MOLLY GREY CRUISE SHIP COZY MYSTERY

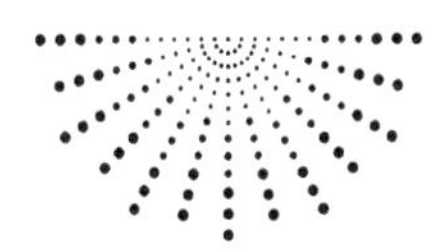

DONNA DOYLE

PUREREAD.COM

CONTENTS

Chapter 1 1
Chapter 2 14
Chapter 3 35
Chapter 4 51
Chapter 5 74
Chapter 6 97
Chapter 7 112
Chapter 8 130
Chapter 9 151
Epilogue 167

Sign Up To Receive Free Books Every Week 171

CHAPTER ONE

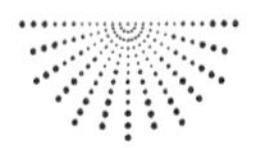

Mace Brick's scowl seemed to be growing by the day. The further he went from his beloved university, the more discontented he became.

To be gone from his important research for a whole month was just too much, and right when he was on the brink of a significant scientific breakthrough. He was sure he was about to uncover the mysteries and the origin of dark matter, but of course Hazel didn't care. She only cared about herself and her own plans, and had virtually made it impossible for Mace not to come on this voyage. She had arranged everything behind his back. Hazel had invited all the guests, most of whom he didn't like, and she had threatened to make a big stink if he would not come.

Now his good name was at stake. Just the kind of publicity he did not need at this moment.

He stared at his papers that were sprawled out before him on the spacious writing desk and let out a frustrated grunt. Then his eyes were drawn again to the half-empty whiskey glass standing right next to his work.

On days like this it appeared whiskey was his only friend, although something in his heart kept telling him he was drinking too much, and he should slow it down.

Well, later he would.

When this journey was over, when Geoffrey was happily married, and he was back at the university; then he would slow it down. Maybe he would even stop drinking altogether, but not now. Not on this wretched cruise.

He picked up his glass, and after he had taken another sip he sloshed the benumbing liquid around in his mouth. Outside of his window, he had to admit, the view was gorgeous. Today, the ocean was almost tranquil. It sparkled in the evening sun, and lit up everything as if they were sailing over a sea of golden honey with hardly a wave to disturb the peace.

No earthly beauty and no amount of whiskey could lighten his frustrated mood. Imagine what a tragedy it would be if Carl Bloomington, that incompetent assistant of his, were to finalize *his* work and get all the credit.

No, he didn't want to be here, on this ship, and it appeared that most of the people Hazel had invited on this cruise didn't want him to be here either. The two nights they had been on their way, especially around dinner time, the tension had been thick as a brick. Hazel would wear that ugly scowl on her powdered face (a glare that now seemed to have become a permanent part of her life), most of the others would stop their so-called happy chatter when he made his appearance, and conversations became strained and collected. And then to think that he was paying for the whole ordeal.

A knock on the door shook him out of his reverie.

"Yes, who is it?" Mace moaned.

"It's me, Dad," came the youthful voice from behind the door.

"Come in, Geoffrey," Mace replied. He finished his whiskey in one gulp and placed the glass back on his desk with an unsteady hand.

Geoffrey was a young man in his early twenties, who had lost the initial traces of youth on his face. Generally, his smile came with ease, but today there was no smile as he entered. His blue eyes, usually so full of zest, flickered with the light of uncertainty. "Hello Dad," he said, and he adjusted the glasses on his nose, a nervous habit he had developed long ago in his youth. "Are you coming for dinner? The bell rang over fifteen minutes ago, and we are all waiting."

"I'm not coming," Mace answered. "I'm not feeling well."

Concern flashed over Geoffrey's face. "Please, do not get sick, Dad. Not now when we are about to reach the island."

"I *am* getting sick, Geoffrey," Mace snorted. "Sick of this cruise, sick of the sea, sick of not being at home, and sick of our guests and the constant complaints of your mother." He hissed in frustration and leaned over to the floor to pick up his whiskey bottle. "I think I'll skip dinner tonight."

"Hazel is not my mother, Dad," Geoffrey replied while his jaws tightened. "Please don't call her mother. At least not when we are in private."

Mace looked up and curled his lip. "She *is* your

mother as far as the world is concerned, and to be very frank, your real mother is not a light in the darkness either, is she?"

"I didn't come here to argue with you," Geoffrey stated in a flat tone of voice. "I just came to tell you we are having smoked salmon crisps; your favorite, and I'd like you to be there."

"No!" Mace fired back, "I am *not* coming. I need to keep my mind on my research, and it doesn't help to allow my mind to be filled with the shallow thoughts of those superficial leeches that are only interested in my money and in having a good time."

"You are drinking too much, Dad," Geoffrey retorted. "You are not making any sense."

Mace's eyes flashed. "Of course I drink, and I am making lots of sense. What do you think? While I should be back home finalizing my research, I am stuck on a boat hundreds of miles from sanity, surrounded by nothing but sea turtles and storms."

Geoffrey's face dropped. "You know this journey means so much to me and Evelyn, Dad. This is supposed to be a highlight of my life. Can't you at least be happy for me and Evelyn?"

Mace narrowed his eyes. "I *am* happy for you,

Geoffrey. I am very happy, although, as you know, I don't care much for Evelyn. But it's your life, and if you want to marry an airhead like Evelyn, be my guest. Marriage is serious business."

"Says the man who is about to divorce his third wife," Geoffrey fired back.

Mace blinked. That was a blow below the belt, but coming from Geoffrey he should let it pass. "Call it experience," he spoke at last, while he poured himself another drink. "At least I know the pitfalls of marriage and I know what I am talking about."

Geoffrey pressed his lips together. "Sorry Dad, I shouldn't have said that. All I am asking is if you would just grit your teeth, appear happy, and do this for me. Think about others for once."

Mace's eyes darkened. More anger. His son was clearly being influenced by Hazel's disrespectful, rebellious attitude. "What are you saying?" he bellowed like a wounded lion, "Are you suggesting I am a selfish man? I think about others all the time. Why do you think I am on this boat in the first place? All my life I've been thinking about others. I've been working hard so I could get you your education, and so I could pay for your mother's expensive shenanigans."

"Hazel's not my mother," Geoffrey said again, this time with a sigh. "You never helped my real mother financially. As far as I know you never even paid her a penny after you kicked her out."

Mace gritted his teeth. Another blow below the belt. Geoffrey's disrespect, coupled with the powerful influence of the whiskey made him raise his voice, and he shouted it out. "I-never-wanted-this-cruise." His outburst almost sounded like the war cry from an uncivilized Barbarian general, who ordered his troupes to march on Rome, and Mace even realized he needed to calm down. After all, Geoffrey wasn't to blame. He licked his lips and added more whiskey, "Sorry son, but you have no idea how hard it is for me to be away from Bright Bricks University... if this journey isn't going to kill me, I don't know what will."

He finished his drink and realized his head was real drowsy. It was as if someone had thrown a wet blanket over his thoughts and he couldn't think straight. Maybe he needed to lie down. His energy seemed to drain out of him and Mace felt flabby and spent. If a bicycle tire had any feelings, this most certainly would be how the tire felt after it had cruised over a couple of broken wine bottles. Just the stress of it all. How nice it would be if he could just lie down…

"Look on the bright side, Dad," Geoffrey spoke in an overly encouraging voice, "This cruise is supposed to calm you down, and the island Hazel has selected for our wedding seems to be a real paradise. I've heard the Captain say that there is nothing like it. Its shores are dazzling, the waters are warm and crystal clear, and we are right in the middle of the Indian Ocean. There are coral reefs, we can go scuba diving, surfing… Just forget about Bright Bricks, Dad, and enjoy life for a change."

"I-I… I don't know," Mace replied and he began to rub his forehead. A headache was working its way in. "I think I need to lie down."

"So… no food?" Geoffrey still tried.

"No food, son," Mace answered as he got up. "I think I am really getting sick."

Geoffrey shook his head, his face a mixture of disdain, frustration and sorrow. "Do us and yourself a favor and stop drinking, Dad," he said as he turned around while Mace threw himself down on the large double bed in the corner of his cabin.

But Mace didn't answer anymore. He closed his eyes

and tried to make sense of the turbulence in his head.

After Geoffrey had walked out Mace tried to make sense of everything his son had said, but for some reason he just couldn't think straight anymore. What was worse, his headache was fast approaching and seemed to take over his head, relentless and cruel like an evil swarm of angry wasps. He had no defense.

Didn't he have an Advil somewhere tucked away in his cupboard?

With difficulty Mace pushed himself up and swung his legs over the edge of the bed. *Steady, Mace... Steady...*

Once he had found his balance he stumbled forward towards the cabin cupboard right next to his desk. When he reached it, (that was quite a feat as he was now staggering violently) he grabbed the wooden top and leaned against it, trying to gather his strength. But he had hardly any strength left, and with a dull, sickening sense of befuddled clarity it dawned on him he wasn't even able to unscrew his bottle of painkillers. Maybe Geoffrey was right and he *was* drinking too much.

The door opened again.

Mace could hear that peculiar creak the door always made. Thank God, Geoffrey had come back. He could help him to get his Advil.

"G-Geoffrey," he cried out. "C-Can you help me get my pa-pain kil-killer. I ca-can't remember where they are."

There was no answer.

"G-Geoffrey?" Mace cried out again, but again, there was no answer. He wanted to turn around and look to see who was coming in, but he just couldn't. It felt so much better to just rest his weary head against the cold wood of the cupboard.

Even in his befogged and stupefied state he sensed someone was approaching. Soft and agile, slithering like a snake. Maybe it wasn't Geoffrey who had entered. After all, Geoffrey never entered without knocking. Then it was Hazel. She didn't have to knock, since this was her cabin too. She must have come down to torment him again about his absence at the dinner table. "Ho-Hon-Honey, I-I am not feeling so good. C-Can you get me my pulls...pills?"

Whoever it was that had entered his cabin was now standing close behind him. "Hazel?" He tried to turn his head but unexpectedly his head was rudely jerked back so he couldn't see, and at the same time he felt something was draped around his neck. "St-Stop this foolishness."

But what happened next startled him. That something that was draped around his neck was Hazel's shawl and it was fast being tightened. In a flash Mace recognized the material. It was that Shahtoosh shawl, that thing she had bought for herself while they had been visiting Kashmir some ten years ago in the days when their relationship was still bearable. But these hands didn't feel like the manicured hands of his wife Hazel, whose nails would pinch deep into his arms on those moments she would be delivering another one of her sermons about his failures as a man. They were not the gentle hands of his son Geoffrey either, hands that would respectfully hold him steady while searching for Advil...,

"St-Stop," he yelled. "I-I don't need a sc-scarf. I need an Advil." But the shawl was not being removed at all. Someone was trying to choke him. He was being attacked. This was no joke. Somebody was out to hurt him.

"Hazel, if that's you, stop it!" he gurgled. He mustered all of his strength in a desperate effort to turn around and push away whoever it was that was standing behind him, but he could barely move. His arms felt like they were filled with raspberry jam. While the shawl pressed deeper and deeper into his neck, and the air was pushed out of his lungs, he could hear the rapid breathing of his assailant. "Air," he gasped, "Pl-Please, I need air."

No answer.

There was only that nauseating, raspy breathing on his neck and the ever tightening grip of that shawl. "I-I'll give you a mi-million dol-dollars. I-I won't tell the po-police." Mace knew these could very well be his last words, but he hoped he could appeal to his attacker's greed. But as the words left his mouth he realized his desperate cry was nothing but an ultimate, meaningless effort. The attacker only squeezed harder.

He was going to die.

He had come to the end of life's road. This was it. Soon the newspapers would carry the story. "Well-known scientist Mace Brick murdered at sea."

But who was doing this to him? There were plenty of folks that disliked him, but who would hate him enough to kill him? In one last violent effort he jerked himself loose and was able to turn around, coughing and wheezing. The world was spinning around as if he was caught in a violent tornado. "W-Who are you?"

With a shock he stared into the eyes of his aggressor. They were blue, just as blue as Hazel's... Then a heavy object was planted on his head and all became blurry and black. Mace fell to the ground.

It was the last thing Mace Brick did on this earth.

CHAPTER TWO

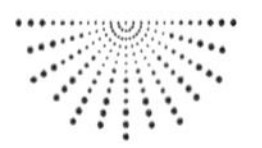

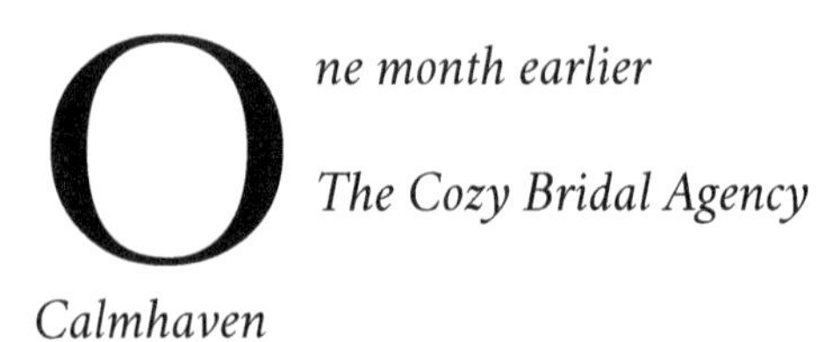

One month earlier

The Cozy Bridal Agency

Calmhaven

Molly Gertrude leaned back in her chair and sipped at her cup of Raspberry-Ginger tea. To her, this was just about the best part of the day. Work was done, a good crime novel in her hands (She had just started The Dagger With Wings by her favorite author G.K. Chesterton) and her best friend and co-worker, Dora Brightside, sitting in the comfortable recliner chair beside her.

As was their custom, after their work at the Cozy Bridal Agency was done for the day, Dora would drive Molly Gertrude back home in her second hand Kia Rio. And there, at Molly Gertrude's comfy home, the two friends would sit together for an hour or so, sipping tea, eating cookies and reading a good book.

At such times it seemed life couldn't be much better. A blessed peace hung over the small living room like a warm, cozy blanket, and all was as it should be.

Or was it?

Lately, a certain restlessness had come over Molly Gertrude, and the old sleuth knew what it was. Nothing much had happened lately and to put it in plain terms, Molly Gertrude was a little bored. Reading crime novels, basically the only thing she would do after work, was great fun, and it challenged her inquisitive brain, but it was no substitute for the real thing, which was solving crimes herself. But there was little she could do about it and she just had to take the bad with the good.

She looked up and studied her dear friend Dora. She seemed engrossed in the Calmhaven Sentinel and it seemed a particular article had grabbed her attention. A wide grin appeared on her face and her eyes sparkled and gleamed. She pushed her nose even closer to the article.

"Anything of interest?" Molly Gertrude queried.

Dora did not seem to hear Molly Gertrude, and mumbled to herself, "Amazing... That's just amazing." She reached over to the coffee table, took another cookie from the tray and expertly broke the delicacy in two. Molly Gertrude chuckled. Her homemade Silky Citrus Curd Cookies were Dora's absolute favorite, and she never failed to eat a few too many. "What, Dora?"

"Wish I could be there," Dora muttered without looking up, as her attention was fully focused on her article again.

"Wish you could be where, dear?" Molly Gertrude inquired, this time a little louder than before.

At last, Dora looked up and while her eyes shone with tiny lights of excitement, she pointed to the newspaper. "l'Ile du Fondu. *That* would be my dream."

"What is Lille de Fondue?" Molly Gertrude asked and arched her brows. "Is there a new restaurant opening up in Calmhaven?"

"No, Miss Molly Gertrude," Dora chuckled. "I am talking about an Island in the Indian Ocean. It's talking about that place in this article here in the

Calmhaven Sentinel, and you will never guess who wrote the article?""

"Oh?" Molly Gertrude stated somewhat flatly. "I have no idea. Somebody we know?"

Dora gave her a small nod. "Remember that journalist that wanted to do an interview on you? That blond fellow who was trying to make a name for himself?"

Molly Gertrude narrowed her eyes as she was searching around in her memory cabinet. At last she gave a short nod. "Are you talking about that fellow that was following us around like a puppy dog while we solved the murder of Albert Gravel? I remember him. His name was Irvin or Herbert or something like that.*

"Virgil," Dora said with a grin. "You never got his name right. His name was Virgil Shepherd."

"Right," Molly Gertrude replied. "Irvin, Herbert... what does it matter? What about him? I thought he became a novelist or something."

"It doesn't seem that way," Dora replied, "Apparently he is back, working for the Calmhaven Sentinel, as this article carries his name."

Molly Gertrude grinned. "I never thought that boy

would make a good novelist, but he was a kind fellow. As I recall, he was mostly interested in our sleuthing business. Is that article about a crime?"

Dora laughed. "No, Miss Molly Gertrude, not at all. Not everything is about crime. But it's still an interesting article for us since it's all about a wedding."

"Oh," Molly Gertrude stated again and wiped a piece of lint from her dress. "Another one of those, huh? Probably another how-to manual, right? One of those *How to get married in five simple steps.* I hate those articles." She wrinkled her nose. "Nowadays everything, including marriage, has to be done fast, furiously and in a flash, but the results are fleeting and feeble. Everyone claims to know the way to happiness and how to live. *Three easy steps to wealth. Healthy and Wealthy in two days..."* Molly Gertrude grunted. "It's just nonsense, Dora. People listen to the advice of the psychiatrist, the baker around the corner, or the weatherman on the TV, but they refuse to listen to their own hearts or to God. Sometimes I wonder what this world is coming to."

Dora clucked her tongue. "You are a bit moody tonight, Miss Molly Gertrude. Are you all right?"

Molly Gertrude drew a deep breath and blew it out

again. "I am sorry, Dora. You are right. I *am* a bit grumpy today, and of course, I have no reason to be cranky. Things could hardly be better for us. Forgive me."

Dora tilted her head. "Then why are you cranky?"

The old sleuth pressed her thin lips together and stared helplessly at her co-worker. "I am just a little bored, Dora. We haven't had much action lately. Sure, the Cozy Bridal Agency was involved in the wedding of John and Lisa Carpenter, and we were asked to do the catering for JJ Barnes and his police ball, but it's been quite some time since we have had some *real* action. There has not been any crime to speak of lately."

Dora frowned. "Shouldn't we be thankful for that? I know your real passion is solving mysteries, but maybe we should be thankful when there are no crimes to solve. After all, crime is no fun, especially for the victims."

"I guess so," Molly Gertrude sighed. "It's just that solving mysteries gives me such a rush. But, you are right. I will try to be more positive. Tell me what that article in the Calmhaven Sentinel, that you think is so amazing, is about?"

"Sure," Dora grinned. "I'll read to you from the works

of Virgil Shepherd." She picked up the newspaper and began to read.

The Stuff Dreams Are Made Of

By Virgil Shepherd

Well-known scientist and millionaire Mace Brick from Pittsburgh and his wife Hazel, known in literary circles for her novel The Undertaker's Nightmare (You may remember the book received the Damaged Plumb award for worst novel of the year) are off to the idyllic island of l'Ile du Fondu in the Indian Ocean."

"Mace Brick?" Molly Gertrude's eyes widened. "I think I've heard of him." She closed her eyes for a moment and thought deeply. "Yes," she spoke at last, "I know who that is. In fact, his grandmother was my science teacher in Junior High."

"She was? How do you know it's the same family? Brick is quite a common name."

"Not really," Molly Gertrude responded. "My teacher, Miss Emily Brick had a grandson named Mace. He was still in diapers at that time. I remember him, because my friends and I went to her house once for a special student evening, and that baby was constantly whining. He pretty much ruined our evening."

"And you think that's the same Mace?"

"Positive," Molly Gertrude declared. "It even says there he's from Pittsburgh. Remember, that's where my ancestor originally started the Cozy Bridal Agency."

Dora pressed her lips together and mumbled. "What a coincidence that you would even know the man."

"I know a lot of people," Molly Gertrude said with a grin, "but what I do not know very well is the geography of the world. Where is that place called l'Ile du Fondu? I have never heard of it before. Is that a big place?"

"I don't know," Dora answered and she pressed her lips together. "But I can google it. She pulled out her smartphone, pushed several buttons and studied the screen for a few seconds. Then she arched her brows and said, "l'Ile du Fondu is French, and it's very small. It's only about 10 square miles, but is apparently a haven for the rich and famous. It houses some of the world's best hotels, has a casino, and is considered one of this earth's most luxurious holiday resorts."

"I thought you said the article is about a wedding?" Molly Gertrude objected.

"It is," Dora said. "Just listen."

Mace Brick, who has been working for years on unraveling the secrets of the mysterious substance known as dark matter, and who claims he's on the verge of making a scientific breakthrough, has lovingly decided to put a temporary stop to his research in order to place the happiness of his family before his career. For there, on the beautiful island of l'Ile du Fondu, their much beloved and only son and his wife-to-be will tie the knot.

"I see," Molly Gertrude said. "Mace is no longer a whiney baby, and now his own son is getting married."

"And *what* a wedding it will be," Dora added. She looked up with dreamy eyes. "Mace Brick is on the Forbes 400 list. I suppose the weddings we plan with our Cozy Bridal Agency look more like a meeting on Skid Row compared to what the Bricks are planning." Dora let out a long sigh. "The rich and famous," she muttered at last, "can do whatever they want."

Molly Gertrude shrugged her shoulders. "Maybe so, but their money cannot buy them true happiness. Money can help you to travel almost everywhere, even to l'Ile du Fondu, but for your journey to heaven it is hopelessly insufficient."

Dora chuckled. "Still, I wouldn't mind taking a peek at that island."

"Read on," Molly Gertrude asked. "What else does that article say?"

To the Bricks only the best is good enough for their son as they and their carefully selected guests, will embark shortly on the cruise ship El Vivo and sail the ocean blue for a dream wedding on l'Ile du Fondu. It has been rumored that—

Miss Molly Gertrude's phone rang. Loud, insisting and demanding and interrupted Dora's reading. Molly Gertrude frowned. "Who could that be? It's after working hours."

"Come on," Dora coaxed, "pick it up before they hang

up. I told you a thousand times you need to get a smartphone. It's so much easier."

"You know I hate those silly devices," Molly Gertrude murmured. "You young people always want things so fast that you are in danger of forgetting yourselves." She forced herself out of her chair and waddled towards the phone that was standing on the little table right under the painting of Molly Gertrude the First, the lady who had originally started the Cozy Bridal Agency somewhere around 1860.

"Hello," Miss Molly Gertrude spoke as she picked up the receiver of the dial phone. "This is the Molly Gertrude residence."

At first it was hard to hear. The connection was crackling and whatever words came through were blaring in her ear. Molly Gertrude did not like the caller. His voice was snooty and demanding as if he were in charge of an army, but at last it seemed the connection was getting better and she understood.

The man was calling for the Cozy Bridal Agency.

Dora stared at Molly Gertrude with curious eyes and whispered, "Who is it?"

"A client," Molly Gertrude whispered back, but

turned her face away as she needed to concentrate on the voice on the phone.

At last she understood what the man wanted. Indeed he wanted them for a wedding, and he promised her it would be well worth the effort... but no, she was not interested. When she had heard all the details, she shook her ageing head in a resolute manner and said, "Sorry, but we are not interested. We are fully booked."

"What do you mean," Molly Gertrude heard Dora howl from behind. "Our agenda is empty..."

Molly Gertrude blushed while she tried to end the conversation with the caller. She understood Dora's dismay and she hated to disappoint her good friend, but this job was a job she would rather not do.

The caller tried one last time and said in his posh voice, *"I'll give you time to think about it. If you change your mind, you can still call me tomorrow morning. I hope we can count on you."*

"That won't happen," Molly Gertrude stated with a firmness she did not feel. "Thank you for calling, and all the best to you."

Molly Gertrude sighed and put the receiver back on

the hook. She looked up at Dora and shook her head again. "There's no way I am going to do that."

"What?" Dora almost shouted it out. "What sort of job was it that you turned it down?"

Molly Gertrude waddled back to her chair and when she sat down she blew out some air. It was going to be hard to convince Dora she had made the right decision by turning this job down. "Funny coincidence…," she began, "…that you were just reading about that in the Calmhaven Sentinel."

Dora froze. "Y-You mean this call was about that wedding feast at l'Ile du Fondu?"

"Yes," Molly Gertrude stated simply. "It was." Her tone was as nonchalant and casual as she could muster, almost as if Dora had asked her if the man who was supposed to read the gas meter had already come by. "It was Mace Brick's secretary."

"M-Mace Brick's secretary called you?" Dora jumped up out of her seat and hovered over Molly Gertrude. "What did he want?"

"Not much," Molly Gertrude answered. "He asked if the Cozy Bridal Agency was willing to arrange the details of a wedding feast."

"What wedding feast? Don't tell me he was talking

about the one in l'Ile du Fondu." Dora, usually a picture of respect and affection for the old sleuth hissed out the words.

Molly Gertrude had expected as much. Of course, to Dora such a job seemed like a golden opportunity. "Yes, Dora," she said at last. "That's the one. Mace Brick wants us to arrange the wedding for his son on that island, l'Ile du Fondu." Molly Gertrude shook her head. "But that's not going to happen."

"Y-You are not serious, are you?" Dora stammered. "Tell me you are joking."

Molly Gertrude looked up. "No, Dora. I am not joking. I will not take that job." How could she explain to her co-worker that she was terrified of the sea? Ever since she had fallen off that yacht when she was five years old that was one fear she had not yet overcome. She had even been wearing a life jacket that day, but she could still hear her father's terrified screams. "Molly Gertrude is overboard! Somebody save her!" The poor man was as terrified as Molly Gertrude herself and seemed frozen into inactivity. All he could do was scream. And Molly Gertrude screamed too. "Help! Help!" Her desperate, high-pitched five year old voice must have carried far and wide over the dark waters that seemed to have one single message for her. "Welcome, little girl...," they grinned at her with their sloshy, watery smiles, "we will take you down to the belly of the sea where you will be food for the lobsters and the catfish."

Of course, she would probably not have drowned that day because of her life-jacket, but neither she nor her father remembered that in the hour of misery. After all, fears are never logical, but always feel very real.

But then, at the moment when Molly was sure the end was near, a pair of strong hands, seemingly coming out of nowhere, grabbed her firmly by her waist and lifted her up out of the waters. A young man, sailing on a nearby boat, had apparently heard Molly's desperate cries and jumped in. Molly would never forget the kind face, but what that man said after she, dripping and miserable, stood next to her Daddy again and mumbled a words of thanks, made even more of an impression on her. The young man had looked at her with a gentle smile and then spoke the words that had become engraved on her heart. They became the motto of her life. He said, "You are welcome, little girl. Just make sure you were *worth* saving."

"But why do you not want to take such a good job,

Miss Molly Gertrude?" Dora's eyes were suddenly big and round. They seemed watery. Poor Dora.

"It's just not possible, Dora." Molly Gertrude stared at Dora's surprised face and knew Dora wasn't going to be satisfied with such a weak explanation. "The Bricks had hired someone, but it turns out that person was a crook and tried to cheat them. So they are looking for a replacement."

"And?"

"They must have heard we were reliable, trustworthy wedding planners."

"I guess that's good news," Dora said, trying to see the good in the situation. "Our name is spreading, Miss Molly Gertrude." Dora licked her lips. It was clear she wanted to hear more.

"Somehow Mace Brick must have found out I knew his grandmother, and they called us," Molly Gertrude continued. "But to make a long story short, I declined. For obvious reasons."

A bewildered expression appeared on Dora's face. Her hand flew up and she grabbed her forehead. "But Miss Molly Gertrude... We would be able to go on a cruise... We could see the world. We would be able to roam the white sands of l'Ile du Fondu, and would be making a fortune in the process… And you talk about obvious reasons to not go on such a trip. What reasons might those possibly be?"

"I-uh…I…" Molly Gertrude stammered. Suddenly she felt tired. Maybe it would be best if Dora would leave. "I-I am not made for the sea, Dora. Can you imagine an old woman like me on a cruise? What if I get seasick?""

"You declined a job to go to l'Ile du Fondu because you are afraid of a little nausea?" Dora let out a yelp and fell back on her chair. "Couldn't we have at least talked about it, Miss Molly Gertrude? And that after you just told me you are a little bored…"

Molly Gertrude lifted her right index finger and stated, "Crime, Dora. I was talking about the absence of crime. Not about having to go up and down on the turbulent waves in the belly of a stuffy ship."

"The El Vivo is not a stuffy ship, Miss Molly Gertrude. It's one of the best cruise ships around. Imagine the fun we would have, not to speak of the money such a job would generate. We could expand our business… maybe even get a better office. And there are pills against seasickness."

"It's not just seasickness, Dora. There's more."

"What?"

"It's the sea, Dora... The sea is so big and deep."

Dora let out another yelp. "You are afraid of the sea?"

"Not much," Molly Gertrude said and her face reddened. "Just a little bit."

Dora leaned back in her seat. "But Miss Molly Gertrude, you are as safe on the El Vivo as in this house. Nothing can go wrong."

"Of course things can go wrong," Molly Gertrude fired back. "What if I fall overboard, and have you seen that movie with Leonardo da Vinci when he was on the Titanic? That movie gave me nightmares."

"His name was Di Caprio," Dora chuckled, "Da Vinci lived long ago. But that was very different," Dora argued, "In those days ships weren't as safe as they are today."

Molly Gertrude rubbed her forehead. She swallowed hard and then told Dora all about her experiences when she was a little girl. When she was done Dora blew out a long puff of air, and at last said, "I never knew that, Miss Molly Gertrude."

"Now you do," Molly Gertrude said barely audible.

Both women were silent for some time, but at last Dora broke through the stillness. "But we should not be chained by our fears, Miss Molly Gertrude. You said so yourself. You are always telling people to have faith in God."

"That's different," Molly Gertrude fired back, but as the words left her mouth she realized Dora wasn't going to accept that statement.

"Nonsense," Dora argued. "The disciples of Jesus were saying the same thing when they too were in a boat and the storm was raging around them. But then Jesus rebuked the winds and the sea, and there was a great calm.' ** If God is on our side, won't he pull us through?"

"I-uh… of course He will," Molly Gertrude spoke while she stared at the floor. "Still, it's sometimes hard to… put that faith into practice."

Dora leaned forward and took Molly Gertrude's hand in hers. "Maybe you don't have crimes to solve, but there are other challenges for us, Miss Molly Gertrude. How about trusting God for a voyage on the ocean blue?"

Molly Gertrude stared at the floor and did not speak for the longest time. At last she looked up again.

"You really think so, Dora? I mean, it would be nice to no longer be afraid of the sea."

"Of course I think so," Dora said. "God can take your fears away in a jiffy, but he won't do it unless you put Him on the spot."

Molly Gertrude looked at her dear friend. So much younger than she was, and yet, at times she simply seemed wiser than she was herself. "You are right, Dora," she said at last. We are wedding-planners, and there's a wedding to be planned. Such opportunities rarely knock twice. I should not yield to my fears like that and be such a scaredy-cat. What's more, we've got no other pressing engagements."

A throaty laugh escaped from Dora's mouth. "Oh, Miss Molly Gertrude, it will be a voyage we will not easily forget."

"Whatever happens, I am sure of that," Molly Gertrude replied in a small voice. Dora's eyes sparkled, but then a thought hit her, and a shadow passed over her face. "But... can we still *get* the job? You told Mace Brick's secretary that you don't want it."

"We can," Molly Gertrude said. "He told me I can think it over and we have till tomorrow. All I have to do is give him a ring at his Pittsburgh office."

"Wonderful," Dora cried out. "In that case I am going home to do some packing."

"Just a minute," Molly Gertrude said while she raised her left hand in an effort to slow Dora down. "Can you please Google the phone number of Brick's office in Pittsburgh? I have no idea how to find his number. Maybe it's time I get myself one of those smart-phones too."

Dora burst out laughing. "You are making enormous progress, Miss Molly Gertrude Grey. Away with all the old, stale fears of the past. We open the gates to the future and welcome the new."

Molly Gertrude forced her face into a smile, but as she did, she realized it must have looked rather fake. "Dear God," she whispered to herself, "Will you please hold my hand? I need you more than ever."

* Read "The Gravel Case"

** Matthew 8:25

CHAPTER THREE

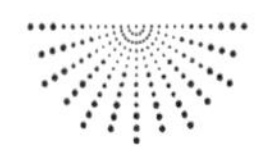

E*mbarking*

Oyster Bay Port

The journey by train from Calmhaven to Oyster Bay Port, the harbor from which the cruise ship, El Vivo, would leave, was rather uneventful, although not as peaceful as Molly Gertrude had wanted. She had hoped to catch up on a bit of sleep, but Dora just wouldn't stop talking and kept on chattering about the wonders of the El Vivo and the journey to come. A five-year-old, going to her long awaited birthday party, would not have been more excited. And at last some of her enthusiasm spilled over on the old sleuth as well. Who knows, maybe Dora was right and this was indeed going to be a wonderful voyage, one they would not easily forget.

But when they got off the train, and Molly Gertrude smelled the salt in the air, and heard the sloshing of the waves on the hull of the El Vivo that loomed up before them like a shining, sparkling monster, she broke out into a cold sweat.

That ship would be her house for some weeks to come. Molly Gertrude instinctively looked back to see if she could still hop on the train again and ride back to the safety of her little home in Calmhaven, but the train had already left. She put her suitcase down so she could wipe her forehead and as she stared at the giant beast in front of them, seemingly asleep in the placid waters of Oyster Bay Port, it appeared the ground beneath her feet became as unstable as the waves out in the open sea. Her initial fears stuck their ugly heads up again.

"This is it, Molly Gertrude..." a particularly nasty and authoritative voice spoke to her mind, *"...behold your coffin."*

Dora seemed oblivious to Molly Gertrude's concerns and kept blabbering about the greatness of the cruise ship. "Isn't the El Vivo a beauty, Miss Molly Gertrude? So strong and safe." She glanced at

Molly Gertrude for a moment and then added, "And complete with the latest safety devices, modern lightweight life jackets, rowboats and more of such stuff."

"Really?" Molly Gertrude replied, not being comforted in the least.

"That's right," Dora sang. "Nothing, Miss Molly Gertrude, and I repeat 'nothing' can go wrong on our journey. Follow me, we will board." Without further ado she picked up her suitcase and walked over to the gangplank. Molly Gertrude sighed and bit her lower lip as she stared after Dora.

"This cruise ship is bigger, faster and packed with more amenities than any other ship I've read about," Dora croaked over her shoulder while she stepped onto the gangplank. Aren't you coming?"

Molly Gertrude hesitated. *Once I am in there, there's no way out.*

"Need any help, Mrs.?" came a voice from behind.

Molly Gertrude turned her head and stared into the bright green eyes of a long-haired man whose head was covered with a wide brimmed hat. He had an enormous moustache as well, and was dressed like a regular cowboy. Not quite the type of person you would expect on a cruise ship for the rich and famous.

"It's Miss," Molly Gertrude replied while she blinked her eyes. "Not Mrs. Are you getting on board as well?"

The man grinned, which caused the wings of his moustache to go up and down. "I was planning to," he said with a Spanish accent. "My name is Carlos Manual Ureña... you know *the* Carlos Manual Ureña." He waited and tilted his head a bit to the side.

Molly Gertrude frowned. "Oh. And what does that mean?"

The man forced a smile on his face. "You never heard of me? Muy Bien. I came in second in American Idol last year... Should have won, but the jury was pretty incompetent. Still, I was second." His face lit up. "Next year I am competing again." He stared for a moment at Molly Gertrude as if he was hoping the light of understanding would yet enlighten the landscape of Molly Gertrude's mind, but nothing came. In fact, Molly Gertrude was more confused than ever, not in the least because she had a healthy dislike of idols. Carlos shrugged his shoulders and repeated his question. "Want me to carry your luggage?"

"Please," Molly Gertrude said at last. "It's most gentlemanly of you."

Carlos nodded and bent over to pick up Molly Gertrude's suitcase. "Glad I can help. You remind me of my grandmother. God bless her soul," he continued as he began to walk towards the ship. "

"Are you one of the guests too?" Molly Gertrude asked.

Carlos stopped and gave her another one of his smiles. "No, Ma'am. Not a guest… I am the entertainer here."

Molly Gertrude's eyes widened. "Entertainer? I don't understand."

"I sing. I am a singer." And to prove he was the real McCoy he broke out into song right when he was crossing the gangplank. His rich voice blended in with the waves and the chatter of seagulls overhead.

Mi sol tu eres mi sol en mi vida

Quiero dar mi vida por te

My sunshine - You are my sun in my life
I want to give my life for you

Apparently the people that were watching at the quay knew very well who Carlos was as they all started to cheer and shout. A few teenage girls were hysterically screaming and they wanted Carlos' autograph.

What a strange world we are living in, Molly Gertrude thought, but she was thankful for the strong hands of Carlos and followed him on board.

Once on the ship, she carefully felt the ground. It did feel stable. She was now standing on some sort of open atrium and an important looking man stopped Carlos. A grand toothpaste smile seemed to be permanently painted on his face, and he was dressed in a blue naval uniform with a double-breasted tailcoat and gold laced blue trousers. "I'll take it from here, Carlos," he said while he plucked at the standing collar of his uniform. "Go and get yourself ready."

Carlos gave the officer a respectful nod, put down the suitcase, and turned back to Molly Gertrude. "Muy Bien. I'll see you tonight, Miss. I'll be singing

Elvis Presley at dinnertime, but I am doing requests too."

Molly Gertrude gave him a polite smile. "I am looking forward to it, Mr. Ureña." Carlos tipped his hat and walked off. The man in the uniform cleared his throat and demanded Molly Gertrude's attention. Still smiling, he stared at both her and Dora with penetrating brown eyes and said, "You two must be the wedding planners from the Cozy Bridal Agency. Mr. Bricks has asked me to personally accompany you to your cabin."

"Thank you," Molly Gertrude replied. "We are indeed the wedding planners."

The man gave her a small nod. "Let me introduce myself. I am the captain of this cruise ship. My name is Coakes. James Coakes." He extended his hand to Molly Gertrude. The handshake was firm and from his demeanor Molly concluded here was a man who knew his business. James Coakes was no rookie, and that was good to know. After all, this man was the one responsible to safely guide her back to the shore in a few weeks.

"Follow me," captain Coakes said. Without waiting for Molly Gertrude's reply he picked up her and Dora's suitcases and started to walk. As they crossed the open area, Coakes began to explain. "This area," he said, "serves as a central gathering spot for the guests on my cruise ship. It is sort of the central spot on our ship. Once we are out on the ocean and the weather is nice, many splendid activities will be held here. For example, the man you just met, Carlos Manual Uraña, will be singing here, accompanied by our pianist. But there are other activities as well, such as a karaoke, family games and all kinds of exciting activities. Nice huh?"

"Very nice," Molly Gertrude mumbled, not wanting to contradict the captain.

"From here," the captain continued, "you can go down to the lower deck, or up to the upper deck. The upper deck is our pride and joy."

"What's there?" Dora queried.

"Everything your heart desires," Captain Coakes answered solemnly. "On the upper decks, there's our casino, two nightclubs, five bars, the private swimming pool, ten hot tubs, alternative restaurants, buffets and the more expensive cabins for the guests of honor, and of course, our 3D movie theatre.

"Ah," Dora said with a gleam in her eyes. "And that's where we will be going. I can't wait."

Captain Coakes pressed his lips together. "Sorry. You'll be going to the lower deck. The cabins there are quite comfortable as well. The public swimming pool is there, as well as the cabins for the crew. Of course, it's a bit more noisy down there, because the engine room is right next to your cabin, but all in all, it's a good place."

"I see," Dora and Molly Gertrude spoke in chorus. The captain did not react, and after he had taken several more steps he stopped in front of a wide door. "For the cabins on the lower deck we are taking the elevator."

He pushed a button and immediately the doors slid open, accompanied by a soft, computer generated woman's voice that said, "Welcome."

A wide, comfortable elevator, with benches attached to the opposite side, right under a gigantic mirror. Molly Gertrude cringed as she stared at her own image. Beholding her tired face, her wrinkled coat, and her hair all out of shape after the long journey wasn't particularly flattering.

But the captain didn't seem to pay much attention to their appearance. Instead, he tenderly stroked the pinewood sides of the elevator and said, "Nice, huh.

Once we are at sea, soft classical music will be playing here too."

When neither of the women reacted to his statement, he wrinkled his nose and pushed the button that was to lead them to the lower deck, and they gracefully zoomed down.

Soon the doors slid open again.

The captain attempted to step out but he was blocked by the back of a broad-shouldered man who was shouting something at a smaller fellow in front of him. The broad-shouldered man was dressed in what appeared to be a penguin suit. The other man, who had his jaws clenched, looked like a worker, dressed in coveralls with grease stains and a beanie that was pulled all the way over his ears. Somehow, the atmosphere was charged with anger. Whoever these people were, it was clear they were in the middle of a heated argument.

"Just take care of it," the man in the penguin suit still howled. "It's what they are paying you for." The other man rearranged the rather dark glasses on his nose with a frustrated shove, but said nothing. Penguin turned around to enter the elevator, but then realized he was face to face with the captain. His demeanor changed somewhat. "Captain Coakes," he huffed. "How good of you to come down. Just in time." He turned and pointed to the man with the beanie. "Your engineer just told me there's a problem with the Waste Heat Recovery Boiler, and we may be delayed. That's *not* acceptable. I won't stay on this canoe one day longer than was the deal."

Captain Coakes rubbed his forehead. "Don't worry, Mr. Brick. I am sure we can take care of it."

"You better," Penguin hissed. "After all, I am the one paying for this whole voyage. Why don't you get an engineer who knows his business?"

The captain did not react to Penguin's last statement, but instead he put on his toothpaste smile again, and turned to Molly Gertrude and Dora. "Ladies," he said, "may I introduce you to Mr. Brick himself."

Molly Gertrude blinked. *So this is Mace Brick?* All she remembered was that little baby boy in diapers. He had changed. Obviously. But his temper was still just as bad as it had been when he was that spoiled brat in the crib that day, when she had visited his house.

"Hello, Mr. Brick," Molly Gertrude said, and she extended her hand. "We are Molly Gertrude Grey and Dora Brightside from the Cozy Bridal Agency. Your secretary hired us to take care of your son's wedding."

"Hope you are better than this engineer here," he scoffed, but he did take Molly's hand in his. "My grandmother knew your parents or something. I need a stable, trustworthy wedding planner to get this show on the road. Can I count on you?"

"Of course," Molly Gertrude replied. She bit her lower lip and then said, "The wedding will be outstanding, Mr. Brick. I hope to be able to soon talk to your son and his wife-to-be and—"

"You can talk to my wife," he interrupted Molly Gertrude. "She's the one to talk to. You don't need to talk to my son, and most certainly not to that woman he wishes to marry." He cast another angry stare at the engineer and then pushed his way past Molly Gertrude, Dora and the captain. Once in the elevator he sat down on the bench under the mirror. "Now if you'll excuse me," he stated, "I have more important things to do. I would like to go up."

"Of course," the captain said, and respectfully moved out of the elevator.

After the doors had closed and the elevator went up, Dora blew out a puff of air. "Whew, that man is quite a character." It seemed she wanted to say more, but when she saw Molly Gertrude's arched brows and the worried expression on Captain Coakes' face, she said nothing more.

The captain glanced at the engineer. "What's the matter with the Waste Heat Recovery Boiler, Dax?"

The engineer shrugged his shoulders. "I need time, Captain. It's probably nothing, but to be frank, sir, that man really gets my goat."

"Quiet, Dax," the captain fired back. "The client always has the last word. Fix it and make sure the man is as happy as a lark."

Dax nodded. "Yes sir. Of course. I'll take care of it." The engineer turned around and left.

Captain Coaxed shook his head. "Running a cruise ship is not a walk in the park," he sighed, "but let me guide you to your cabin."

The Captain entered a rather dark, narrow passageway and led them to a small door somewhere in the middle. "Your cabin," he said with a pleased expression. He took a key out of his pocket, opened the door, and then handed the key to Molly Gertrude.

It turned out to be a small cabin, no more than twenty by twenty feet, and it was a little stuffy and smelly as well. Molly Gertrude guessed the more distinguished guests would most certainly have better accommodations. At least the porthole could be opened, and that was the first thing Molly Gertrude did after they had entered. The captain walked over to a metal bunk bed on the wall and placed Molly Gertrude's suitcase on the lower bunk. "Well ladies, welcome aboard the El Vivo," he said with a grin. "Maybe this cabin is not the most luxurious one on the ship, but the sleep here is sweet, and of course you are welcome to make use of all the facilities we have to offer."

"Thank you," Molly Gertrude said. "I will remember that."

The captain gave her a small nod. "Departure is scheduled in one hour. Just get settled in, and if you have any questions, feel free to ask me." Without waiting for a response he turned around and left. The door apparently slipped out of his hand and closed behind him with a loud bang. Molly Gertrude heard him mumble a word of apology and then all was still.

Neither Molly Gertrude nor Dora knew what to say. At last, Molly sighed and walked over to the porthole and glanced out. Even though the sea was calm, still it seemed to pulsate with life. Molly Gertrude had not been to the sea very often and the sight of the enormous, never-ending body of water filled her with awe. The water sparkled like diamonds, as the light of the afternoon sun was reflected in the foamy waves. As Molly Gertrude drank in the scene a sense of peace enveloped her. These were going to be difficult weeks, but Dora was right; there was a lot to be thankful for.

But then, just when she wanted to comment to Dora on the beauty of the sea and its restful influence, a terrible noise erupted. The beast had awakened and was now roaring, panting and huffing. It even caused a slight tremble in the very cabin they were in.

"W-What's that?" Dora gasped.

"It's the engine of the ship," Molly moaned. "We are right next to the engine room and we are soon leaving."

"Do we have to hear this noise the whole trip?" Dora stammered. "I can't even hear myself think."

"I am afraid so," Molly Gertrude said. "But in for a penny, in for a pound. We will just have to make the best of it. And don't forget, you really wanted to come on this trip."

Dora blushed. "I-I didn't know they would put us in this lousy cabin."

"Well, this is where we are." Molly Gertrude clucked her tongue. "From now on we will have to trust God that we can do a good job, and we'll be back in Calmhaven in a jiffy. Wasn't it St. Paul who said that we should be content in whatever state we find ourselves in?"

Dora nodded, but by the look on her face it was clear to Molly Gertrude that Dora, in her murmuring state, doubted whether even Paul would have been very happy in the belly of the El Vivo, right next to the engine room, when there were luscious, comfortable cabins, even a few empty ones, on the upper deck.

"Cheer up," Molly Gertrude said. "We are professionals, and as you yourself said, we are about to embark on a voyage we will not soon forget."

CHAPTER FOUR

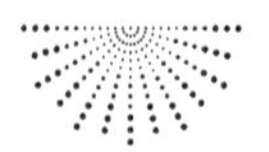

When the foghorn sounded, indicating that the El Vivo was about to take off, a ghostlike figure rose from the bed in the stuffy cabin. Not a real ghost of course, for a real ghost can't be heard to yawn and cackle, but this figure did. Since the small blinds were closed over the porthole, and the lights inside the cabin were turned off, only a vague silhouette could be seen.

The figure had been waiting for the foghorn. The journey would begin and that meant that the last days of Mace Brick were beginning too. Soon the wealthy scientist would be no more, and freedom would knock at the gate. Real freedom and final deliverance from that oppressing yoke. But the cards needed to be played well, for it was important the blame would fall on the chosen subject. Then two flies would be killed with only one stone. A delightful prospect, and it was unlikely the plan would go wrong. If an unsuspecting bystander would have been in the cabin, he would have been appalled by the oppressing sense of darkness that had filled the cabin as the silhouette gave his hatred full reign. But there was no one else there, and the lone figure seemed quite comfortable in the gloomy atmosphere.

The foghorn sounded again. Time to get to work. The silhouette walked towards the door of the cabin and opened it. There was a shiver when the light streamed in. At this stage, darkness was better than light, but that was just the way it had to be. A few more days, a few more moments in the presence of the enemy and then the victory was won...

As soon as the shoreline disappeared from sight and the El Vivo was gently dancing on the soft waves, nausea hit Dora.

"I-I... don't feel so good," she exclaimed to Molly Gertrude while she looked up with weak, helpless eyes.

Molly Gertrude frowned. "What's wrong, dear?" The old sleuth narrowed her eyes as she focused on Dora's face. "Oh, my… you are sick indeed. You are all green. Is it something you ate?"

"No, Miss Molly Gertrude," Dora said with a deep sigh. "I am sea-sick." She sank down in the only chair the small cabin possessed, and hung her head in between her knees while mumbling, "A-Are you s-sick too?"

Molly Gertrude checked the state of her being. Nothing seemed to be wrong with her. Her stomach felt fine and so did her head. Seasickness had been one of her biggest fears, but she hadn't thought of it anymore since they had boarded. "No, Dora, I am not." She almost wanted to apologize and tell Dora she was sorry she wasn't sick as well but, obviously, that was ridiculous. Instead she pointed to the porthole and said, "Fresh air, Dora. Go stand in front of the porthole, it will do you a world of good." But Dora shook her head. "No… I don't want to. C-Can you get me some pills so I can feel good again?"

Molly scratched her head. "I don't have any. Do you have some in your suitcase?"

"No," Dora stammered, "I didn't think I'd get sick.

The Medical Officer on the El Vivo will have some. Will you ask him, Miss Molly Gertrude?"

"And leave you here by yourself, sick?"

"There's nothing else you can do, M-Miss Molly Gertrude. P-Please?"

It was clear Dora had known better days and help *was* needed. Molly Gertrude scanned the small cabin and spotted an empty bucket which she placed near Dora.

"W-What's that for?" Dora mumbled.

"Just in case, dear," Molly Gertrude said with some concern. "In the meantime, I will see if I can get you some pills."

"H-Hurry," Dora moaned.

A minute later Molly Gertrude was back on the wide deck that Captain Coakes had said would be used for fun activities. She marveled as soon as she stepped out of the elevator. When she had gone down to the lower deck with the captain the scene had been one of busy activity, and scores of people milling about on the quay, but how different the view was now. She turned her head in all directions, and while the wind was pulling on her clothes and hair, a sense of awe welled up in her heart. Wherever she looked she saw water. The coast was long gone, and all the way to the horizon there was nothing but the endless pattern of waves canopied by fluffy white clouds and the occasional ray of the late afternoon sun. And then to think that the waters underneath the ship were so deep that no living soul could ever descend there without a special suit, and that no light would penetrate down there. A group of seagulls were soaring by, chattering and clamoring for attention, apparently hoping for some scraps of food. They were so loud that Molly Gertrude concluded the market salesman at the fish market in Calmhaven couldn't be louder. Molly Gertrude followed them with her eyes for a few moments, but then the image of poor, suffering Dora pushed her thoughts back to her mission. She needed to get those pills.

She spotted a man with white, silvery hair not too far away from where she was standing. He was not as old as she was herself, but old enough to be Dora's dad. He was dressed in a costly white summer jacket with matching slacks, but strangely enough, he was just wearing thongs. Just the same kind of flip-flops Miss Annabelle Goodwinkle, Molly Gertrude's hired maid wore when she came once a week to clean her house. But Miss Goodwinkle received Government benefits. She was poor and couldn't afford fancy shoes and had decided she would be just as happy in flip-flops. But on this ship nobody was poor. These people could be wearing diamond studded flip-flops if they so chose.

But since there was nobody else around, she just had to ask him if he knew where she could find the Medical Officer. After all, what did it matter what kind of shoes he was wearing? What *did* matter was whether he knew where Molly Gertrude could get pills for Dora's sickness.

"Excuse me, sir," Molly Gertrude began, after she had walked over to him. The man seemed deep in thought as he was leaning against the railing, and looked out over the ocean. Molly Gertrude almost hated to disturb him as he was no doubt enjoying the view.

The man turned his head and looked at Molly Gertrude. "Hello," he replied warmly. He was a charming fellow. His eyes shone with little lights, and his silvery hair gave him a distinguished appearance. If it had not been for his flip-flops, Molly Gertrude would have guessed he was a banker, a stock broker, or a politician, but now she just couldn't tell. He stared at her for a fraction of a second and then said in a melodious voice, "What's a delightful, attractive lady like you doing on this ship?"

Molly Gertrude blushed. She had not expected such flowery words of admiration. "I-I am an old lady," she mumbled. She wanted to say more, but the flip-flop man gave her no chance and said, "Some people indeed are old. Old in body and old in spirit. But in you I spot something else." He nodded to show he was in agreement with himself, and then continued, "In your eyes I see streams of wisdom springing up from the vaults of experience. The windows to your soul carry an unmistakable beauty. *That*, my dear lady, is a wealth not to be despised."

Molly Gertrude tilted her head to the side. Was this fellow just trying to butter her up? The last time anyone had said admiring stuff like that was so long ago, it was hard to even remember. Most likely, this man was nothing but a smooth talker. An old geezer with his own secret agenda, who had a girlfriend in every port or city, and was used to getting his way with the women.

She needed to be on guard.

"Thank you," Molly Gertrude said in short tones, "but I was just wondering if you could tell me where I can find the Medical Officer?"

"You mean Dr. Biddle?" the man replied.

"Yes, I guess so," Molly replied. "I need him for some pills against seasickness."

The man nodded and then he said, "I'll walk you to his cabin. By the way, my name is Guillermo DaCosta. Professional bachelor." He grinned at his own joke.

"Miss Molly Gertrude Grey," Molly answered politely. "I am a professional wedding-planner, so I guess we won't be much good to each other. Bachelors are not usually on my list of clients."

Guillermo burst out into a hearty laugh. "Not only are you wise and experienced, you have a sense of humor as well. I like that in a lady." He chuckled some more and then said, "Don't worry Miss Grey, not everything in life has to be professional. But come, and I'll lead you to the doctor's cabin." Without waiting for Molly Gertrude's response, he linked arms and guided her back to the elevator.

This time they didn't go down to the lower deck, but now they went up.

When they stepped out of the elevator onto the upper deck Molly Gertrude had to swallow hard. How different this area was from the place she and

Dora had been dumped into by Captain Coakes. Here, everything sparkled and gleamed. The place smelled fresh and clean, and everywhere there was light. Large windows gave a superb view of the sea on both sides, and soft, relaxing music played over strategically placed loudspeakers. In the far end of the spacious place, (Molly Gertrude guessed the place was almost as big as Pastor Julian's church in Calmhaven), was a row of comfortable cabins. Nice cabins, with shiny doors, pretty plants, and old fashioned, silver colored lanterns attached above each individual door. They would no doubt be lit at night and bathe the area in a fairy-like glow. This was what Dora had been dreaming of.

"Dr. Biddle has his office over there," Guillermo said, and pointed to the far end. "He is quite a—"

But he couldn't finish his sentence as the mellow, dulcet voice of a woman interrupted him. "You are too early, Guillermo."

Guillermo DaCosta stopped abruptly and turned. When he saw who had spoken, his face broke out into a wide smile. "Hazel," he proclaimed with a loud voice. "I know I am early, but I am just helping this dear lady."

The woman arched her brows. Something in her

demeanor told Miss Molly Gertrude she was not pleased at Guillermo's enthusiastic response. Guillermo seemed to catch on to it as well. He turned his gaze first to the right and then to the left, almost as if he wanted to make certain nobody was spying on them.

"It's all right, Guillermo," the lady continued. "You don't have to be so skittish. Just don't forget."

"How could I forget?" Guillermo now almost whispered. "You know my heart makes a somersault whenever I see you. You look more ravishing by the day."

Molly Gertrude had to admit the woman was quite attractive. At least, by worldly standards. She was undeniably pretty, with her long, wavy blond hair and slender build. The colorful, sleeveless beach dress with the flower print that she wore could come straight out of Cosmopolitan, and her manners were suave and collected. But there was one thing that Molly Gertrude didn't like. Her eyes were not warm. They smiled, but not in a way that made you feel good. They were hard, cold and cunning, rather than soft and inviting. But Guillermo didn't seem to think so, or didn't show it at least, and continued to shower the lady with compliments, albeit in a whisper. "Your eyes, Hazel, are like the pearls in the Queen of England's collier and—"

"Stop it, Guillermo," the lady tried to look angry, but Molly heard a soft giggle. "Rather tell me what you are doing here."

"I am helping a dear old woman," Guillermo replied, now in his normal voice again. He turned to Molly Gertrude. "Miss Grey, this is Hazel Brick. Hazel this is Miss Grey."

Hazel Brick? She's the wife of Mace Brick.

Molly stared at the woman with renewed interest. So, this was the well-known Hazel Brick, the one who apparently was organizing the whole voyage. She was a lot younger than Mace. Maybe that was to be expected. After all, Mace had been married two times before. Hazel was his third wife, and it seemed Mace was going for looks.

"This dear woman is looking for Dr. Biddle," Guillermo explained. "She is afraid she's getting seasick."

"Oh my," Hazel wrinkled her nose, trying to act interested. "So early on in the journey?"

"It's not for me," Molly Gertrude spoke. "It's for my

associate. You see, we are the wedding planners, and we cannot afford to be nauseous."

Hazel narrowed her eyes. "I thought I recognized that name Grey. So you are the old woman who has been called in to replace the original wedding planner? I have heard good things about you..." She paused and seemed to be studying Molly Gertrude from top to bottom. Then she continued, a bit sharp, "... I hope those stories are all true. These days people seem more interested in making quick money than in doing a decent job."

"We will do our best, Mrs. Brick," Molly Gertrude replied and forced a little smile on her face.

"We will see, won't we?" Hazel answered. "In any case, we have a lot to discuss, you and I." She threw her long, blond hair over her shoulder with a swift move of her hand, causing a whiff of perfume to penetrate Molly Gertrude's nose. "I had been planning to have a meeting with you tomorrow," Hazel Brick continued. "As you may know, I am the wife of Mace Brick, and as such I am your boss."

Molly Gertrude kept on smiling, but inside she labeled Hazel Brick in category 4. *Category 4: Difficult client. Proud, arrogant, selfish. Treat with the utmost caution.* It was best not to cross this woman.

Not now, and not ever, at least not as long as they were stuck on this ship together. Hazel Brick extended her hand and Molly Gertrude shook it. "I'll call for you when I'm ready, it might be a day or two before I get around to you," Hazel said, and then turned her attention back to Guillermo. Molly Gertrude no longer existed. Dora needed to be prepared and instructed, as her young associate still had a bit to learn about staying meek and kind when confronted with unreasonable and demanding clients.

Molly Gertrude noticed Hazel's hand brushing by Guillermo's hand ever so quickly, and Molly Gertrude heard her whisper. "Be on time, Guillermo. Check your watch."

"You know, I don't have one," he whispered back. Hazel stared at him for a moment, but then she turned around, and walked off without saying another word.

When she had disappeared out of sight, Guillermo turned his attention back to Molly Gertrude and said, "Sorry for the interruption. Let's go, I'll get you to Dr. Biddle."

After Guillermo had guided Molly Gertrude to what turned out to be the waiting room of the doctor, he no longer wanted to stay around. "Here it is, Miss Grey," he said. "It's been my pleasure to make your acquaintance, but I've got to go now. I have other obligations. The doctor will be with you shortly."

"Does he know I am here?" Molly Gertrude asked.

Guillermo gave her a small nod. "He's got a camera in his office. Just wait, and he'll be out before you can say Jack Robinson." Having said that he gave Molly Gertrude another one of his charming smiles and made a little bow. "Tonight, after dinner, there's the possibility of dancing. Allow me to be the first one to take you into my arms… eh, I mean, on the dance floor of course."

Molly pressed her lips together. A dance with Guillermo DaCosta? Maybe she should stay in her cabin. "Thank you, Mr. DaCosta, but I am a terrible dancer. Goodbye."

After Guillermo had left, Molly sighed and thought of Dora. By now, the poor girl was no doubt as sick as a dog. It seemed down in the belly of the ship things did not feel nearly as stable as up here on the upper deck. Here, it felt as if she was walking around in the center of Calmhaven.

Happily, it turned out Guillermo had been right as far as the doctor showing up soon. Molly Gertrude had just planted herself in one of the comfy chairs in the waiting room, and grabbed a copy of Reader's Digest from the stack of magazines on the nearby table, when the door to the doctor's office opened and two men appeared.

One of them was sneezing uncontrollably while he had his nose covered with a handkerchief. The other man, who had his hand on the shoulder of the sneezer, said in an authoritative voice, "Three times a day, Silas, and no cutting corners. Mr. and Mrs. Brick need you to be healthy and fit."

The man nodded and answered with another sneeze, right when he was passing Molly Gertrude. The old sleuth ducked away in case the man had a contagious disease. It sure didn't sound very healthy.

The other man, presumably Dr. Biddle, noticed Molly Gertrude's reaction and chuckled. "Don't worry. It's only hay fever," he said, "It's not contagious."

He opened the door to the lounge and pushed the unfortunate sneezer outside and turned his attention to Molly Gertrude. "What can I do for you, Mrs. ...?"

"Miss Molly Gertrude Grey," Molly Gertrude answered. "Are you Dr. Biddle?"

"That's me," Biddle replied, while he stared at her from behind a pair of sunglasses. "Rasheed Biddle. What can I do for you?"

Molly Gertrude hesitated. Rasheed Biddle did not look much like a doctor at all, at least not to Molly Gertrude. His hair was not properly combed and was badly in need of a haircut. In fact, it almost looked like the man had just climbed out of bed, although Molly Gertrude had heard about the so-called wild surfer look. Now she knew how that looked, something which was greatly enhanced by the clothes this man was wearing. The skinny, pale legs of this man, were sticking out of a pair of shorts, and his torso was covered by a Hawaiian flower shirt, of which the top buttons were opened. As a result, Molly Gertrude was forced to study his chest hair, an activity she was not fond of doing. But of course, this was the doctor on a cruise ship where the rich and famous did as they pleased, and where apparently everyone dressed the way they liked.

"I-I was hoping you'd provide me with a pill against sea-sickness."

"Certainly," Dr. Biddle said while he raked his hand

through his black, messy hair. "You're already sick, huh?" he said with a grin. "But I have got just what you need."

"It's not for me," Molly Gertrude explained again for the third time. "It's for my associate. She and I are the wedding planners."

Dr. Biddle raised his sunglasses from his nose so he could take a better look at Molly Gertrude. "So…," he said at last, "…you are the unfortunate lady that has to get this circus on the road?"

Molly Gertrude frowned. "Excuse me?"

Dr. Biddle curled his lips as he took off his sunglasses. His eyes were dark.

"Just between us," the doctor said and he lowered his voice to a whisper, "this whole thing is a crying shame. But as for me, I am just going to make the best of it, and hope this is my last dealing with the Bricks."

Molly Gertrude frowned. "Why? What's wrong? Isn't a wedding a wonderful occasion of love and joy, where two people promise to love each other in the good and the bad times?"

Rasheed Biddle laughed, but it was not a happy laugh. "You are a romanticist, Miss Grey, but in the world that I have witnessed these past years there's no room for such ideas." He sat down on the seat opposite of Molly Gertrude and said with a scowl, "I know the Bricks quite well. I am their family doctor, but believe me, there's not a speck of sincerity and love in that household."

"Oh." Molly Gertrude leaned back in her seat and decided to just listen.

"You know it's their son Geoffrey that's going to get married, right?"

Molly Gertrude nodded. "I have not met him yet but, yes, that's what I heard."

"Geoffrey is not a bad fellow," Biddle continued. "He did not want this cruise. In fact, he wanted to elope with his girl, her name is Evelyn, and have a simple wedding ceremony in a country church." Dr. Biddle shook his head in disgust and sneered, "But Hazel Brick found out about it, and put a stop to the whole deal. You should have seen the fit that woman threw. And you know what they did afterwards?"

Molly Gertrude shook her head.

"They forced Geoffrey's wife-to-be to sign a legal document that cuts her off from any financial benefits. They actually threatened that poor girl, and the Bricks have complete control of their union."

"But how is that possible?" Molly Gertrude asked. "Aren't Geoffrey Brick and Evelyn of age?"

"Of course they are," Dr. Biddle said, "but I don't think Geoffrey even knows about it. If you ask me, I would say either that poor girl is scared out of her wits, or she simply loves Geoffrey so much that she's willing to go along with her wicked, overbearing parents-in law."

Molly Gertrude leaned back. This was simply a horror story. "So, it's going to be a wedding with a lot of unhappy people," she said at last.

"Seems that way," Dr. Biddle replied, "But I don't care anymore. After this trip, I am out of here. I will no longer be their family doctor. I've made my decision, as well as my arrangements for the future."

Molly Gertrude blinked her eyes. "So if you feel this way, then why did you even come on this trip?"

"Money, Miss Grey. It's plain and simple. It's been my longtime dream to set up a children's hospital in my home town. Mace Brick has promised to fund it..."

"That's nice," Molly Gertrude said. "So, apparently Mr. Brick is not altogether bad."

But Dr. Biddle shook his head. "He is, Miss Grey. That man made that promise ten years ago, but he never honored the promise. It's like that silly story my son told me about. A story he heard in Sunday school."

Molly Gertrude looked up. "What story?"

Dr. Biddle let out an uncontrolled moan. "It's a children's story, about a fellow named Jacob. My son told me he was promised a wife if he'd work for his boss for seven years. But that wicked boss kept postponing and postponing, and constantly cheated that man Jacob. I heard he had to work 21 years for that boss of his... I think his name was Lalab or Balam, or something stupid like that. That just about describes my life."

"Laban. His name was Laban." Molly Gertrude chuckled. "Do you believe that story?"

Biddle blushed. "Me? No, of course not. I know better than to believe such stuff, but it's good for my kid. Teaches him good morals and stuff."

"Actually," Molly Gertrude said in a soft voice, "Jacob was a bit of a crook himself, at least until he really found God. I think, Doctor, that finding God is always the key to real success."

Dr. Biddle stared at Molly Gertrude with a blank expression. "I wouldn't know," he said at last. "All I know is, I want Hazel and Mace Brick out of my life." He pressed his lips together and stared at Molly Gertrude with dark eyes. "Did you know," he continued, "there's probably not a person on this ship who actually likes Hazel and Mace Brick?"

Molly Gertrude said nothing. There was nothing she could say.

"Take that man for example who just left my office," Dr. Biddle added. "That was Silas Thorne. He's been their personal florist for years, and he's in charge of the flower arrangements for the wedding. But poor Silas is allergic to Casablanca Lilies. Those particular flowers give him a horrible case of the sniffles. Now you may guess what flowers Hazel Brick has ordered for the wedding?" He leaned forward, almost demanding Molly Gertrude to answer.

"Casablanca Lilies?"

"Yeah," Dr. Biddle snapped. "You just won the jackpot. Hazel Brick doesn't care. She said Silas Thorne just needs to get over it. I tell you, Miss Grey, there's no love in that family. Anyway, Miss

Grey...," he licked his lips, "I have decided to just make the most of this journey, and I will abuse as much of the Brick's so called generosity until I..."

He suddenly stopped and never finished his sentence. Instead he looked at his watch. "Oh my, it's almost dinner time."

"Until you *what,* Doctor?" Molly Gertrude still asked.

"Nothing, Miss Grey. Nothing at all." The doctor got up and walked towards his office. "Just a moment. I'll get you the pills for your unfortunate co-worker." A minute later he returned again with a small cardboard package and pulled out a strip of pills which he handed to Molly Gertrude. "One before breakfast, one before dinner," the doctor said. "No more, because then she'll get nauseous."

Molly Gertrude stared at the strip in her hand. "I thought these pills were to prevent nausea?"

Dr. Biddle sighed. "Just stick to the prescription. Now, if you will excuse me, I need to get dressed for my first meal on the El Vivo."

Molly Gertrude nodded and stuck the pills in her handbag. "Thank you, Doctor," she said and got up as well. "It's been most enlightening."

"You are welcome," Dr. Biddle said. As Molly

Gertrude shook his hand and she looked in the man's eyes, she couldn't help but shiver. His eyes were cold and heartless. Hopefully she wouldn't need medical assistance while on this voyage. This man was not to be trusted and she would have to be very ill before she would consider coming near him again.

CHAPTER FIVE

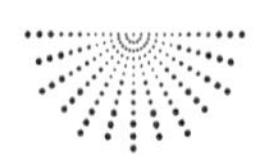

With the pills safely in her handbag, Molly Gertrude waddled back to the cabins on the lower deck as fast as her old legs would let her. Poor Dora was probably beside herself by now, as this whole ordeal had taken almost an entire hour. To Molly Gertrude's relief, finding the elevator again was relatively easy and when she stepped inside she congratulated herself on being so efficient. But just as she pushed the button to go down, the doors of the elevator swung open again, and the slouched figure of the First Engineer appeared.

"Hello," the man in his greasy coveralls said, "Do you mind if I go down with you?"

"No, of course not," Molly Gertrude replied. "You are

Dax, aren't you? The one in charge of the machinery."

Dax, still wearing his beanie, nodded and gave Molly Gertrude a forced smile. "You have a good memory," he said at last while pushing the elevator button. "I am sorry you had to witness that little quarrel I had with Brick."

Molly Gertrude shrugged. "It's nothing, really. That happens in the best of families."

"But I am *not* family," Dax said while he wrinkled his nose. He pushed his dark glasses further up his nose. "And I never will. I don't think that man's mother gave him a very good education. He is rude, self-centered and cunning."

"That's quite a mouthful," Molly Gertrude replied while she stared at Dax in surprise. "I actually know his grandmother. She was a nice lady."

Dax' face flushed. "Sorry," he said. "But as you surely know, it takes more than just one swallow to make a summer."

The doors opened. They had arrived.

As they stepped out, Dax asked, "Are you and that other lady staying in the cabin near the engine room? Sorry for all the noise. They should have given you a better cabin."

"It's all right," Molly Gertrude answered, not wanting to add more fuel to the obvious angry fire that was burning in the man's heart. She changed the subject as they walked towards the engine room and the cabins. "Have you been on this cruise a long time, Mr. Dax?"

He grinned. "Call me Dax. And no, this is my first job as an engineer."

Molly arched her brows. "So you haven't been an engineer most of your life?"

"Nope." Dax shook his head. "I was hoping for a career in science, but it didn't work out to well. So, I switched to engineering. After all, keeping the engine on a cruise ship in tip-top shape is somewhat of a science as well."

Molly Gertrude understood. "Hope it all works out for you," she said, as they now reached the door to Molly Gertrude and Dora's cabin.

"Thank you," Dax said. "Enjoy your wedding." He tipped his beanie in an effort to appear polite and walked on, while Molly knocked on the door. "Dora… open up. I got your pills. Salvation is nigh."

Nobody answered.

Molly Gertrude knocked again, this time so loud, it was more like banging. "Dora! Open up!"

Dax was just about to step into the engine room, but he heard her cries and stopped. "Is everything all right?" he called out.

Molly Gertrude cast him a helpless stare. "My co-worker is seasick, but it appears she is too ill to open the door, and I don't have a key."

"No problem," Dax said with a smile and he walked back to Molly Gertrude. "I'll help."

A second later he stood next to Molly and with a grand smile he pulled out a set of keys. "I have the master key to all doors on this cruise," he said. "Leave it to Dax, everything will turn out all right." He grinned, fiddled with his keys, and after he found the one he was looking for, the door to the cabin opened with a creak.

"I'll see you around," Dax said. He wanted to walk away, but Molly Gertrude grabbed his arm. "Thank you," she said. "I was getting very worried, but you helped."

"No problem," Dax said again. "It's been my pleasure. My dear old mother always said that we are here on the earth to make life as easy as possible for one another. Call on me anytime." Not wanting to lose any more time he walked off and Molly Gertrude stepped inside.

"Dora?"

Still no answer.

Molly Gertrude scanned the room, but there was no sign of her co-worker. Dora was not in the chair she had been sitting in and neither was she on the top bunk. Where could she have gone?

For a moment fear tried to make its entrance in Molly Gertrude's heart. What if Dora was so sick that she had gone outside and had fallen overboard? But as soon as the thought rose, Molly Gertrude pushed it away. Ridiculous. Sick or not sick, Dora Brightside was not stupid. She would just have to wait.

Thus Molly Gertrude sank down in the chair and waited.

And then, just when her eyelids had become heavy, and she was about to drift off to sleep, there was commotion in the corridor, and a second later, Dora appeared.

Molly Gertrude rose up. "Dora… I've got your pills."

"No need, Miss Molly Gertrude," Dora replied in a chirpy voice. She was wearing a smile and had a healthy, rosy color on her cheeks. She did not look sick at all.

"What happened?" Molly Gertrude asked. "You are not sick anymore?"

"All healed," Dora exclaimed. "I don't think I've ever been so sick, but then I remembered that ginger is an excellent remedy against nausea."

Molly Gertrude stared at her blankly. "Where do you get ginger in the middle of the ocean?"

"I forced myself up and dragged my weary body to one of the restaurants," Dora explained. "'Ginger,' I cried when I got there. 'I need ginger.'" She burst out laughing. "They must have thought I was drunk, but luckily for me, I ran into a nice chef, and he had fresh ginger." Dora's eyes lit up as she thought of the man. "He's Swedish. His name is Hampus Rosenqvist, and he's almost as handsome as Digby.* He told me he wants to take me dancing one night..."

Molly Gertrude shook her head. "You should have waited for me, Dora."

Dora gave Molly Gertrude a smile, but it appeared

her grin had a bit of a sharp edge to it. "I *did* wait for you, Miss Molly Gertrude, but you never came back. I figured you had gotten lost, so I had to take matters into my own hands."

Molly Gertrude crossed her arms. "You still should have waited. And since when is ginger such a panacea? Isn't that just a bunch of quackery?"

Dora narrowed her eyes. "Panacea or not; all I know is, that once I was seasick, but now I am fine." Then she continued in a more friendly tone, "But, from now on, I'll be serving you ginger-tea, Miss Molly Gertrude. It's supposed to be very good for arthritis as well."

Molly Gertrude nodded. "Well, in case your ginger runs out, I still have some pills for you." Then she changed the subject and told Dora about her own encounters with the people on board of the El Vivo. When she was done, she let out a long, frustrated sigh. "These are going to be difficult weeks Dora. It seems no-one really likes the Bricks. Organizing this wedding is like navigating through a mine-field."

"We'll manage," Dora said confidently. She tilted her head while squeezing her chin and seemed preoccupied with something else. "Did I bring my dancing shoes? I sure hope so," she mumbled to herself and walked over to her suitcase to check.

Molly Gertrude sighed with exaggeration. Dora's attitude confirmed her fears. Even though they were assigned to this lousy cabin, it seemed Dora too had caught the party-virus that hung over the El Vivo. But this was not going to be a party at all. Molly Gertrude had a strong premonition that things would not turn out all that well. While Dora was rummaging through her stuff and let out a victorious howl when she found her elegant high-heeled pumps, Molly Gertrude sighed. These were going to be difficult weeks indeed.

* Digby is the right-hand man of police-chief JJ Barnes in Calmhaven. Dora and Digby are very fond of each other, although it seems their relationship never seems to be taking off.

"Divorce?" Mace Brick's body tensed. "What are you talking about?" He had been against this voyage from the very beginning, and now this? One month away from his scientific research was a major obstacle, but of course dear Hazel, that prima donna wife of his, couldn't care less and had pushed her own program through, as usual. Also as usual, he had consented to please her… He always did, even to his own hurt. Divorce? What was she talking about? She was nothing but an unthankful wretched wife who was bent on spending his money faster than he could bring it in. He narrowed his eyes and felt the heat flush through his body. "Don't tell me there's another man in your life."

Hazel sat on the edge of their massive, canopied bed in the middle of their spacious cabin, and casually continued to polish her nails. "No, there isn't," she stated in a flat, unconcerned tone, as if a waiter had just asked her if she wanted ketchup with her french-fries. She inspected her red fingernails, blew on them for a moment so they would dry faster, and then looked up into Mace's eyes. "I said, I am *thinking* about a divorce. I am not decided yet. Of course, we should keep this between ourselves for now. But, I will give you one more chance."

She is giving me one more chance? Mace's fists curled up into tight little balls, and he fought hard to control his temper. Nobody divorces Mace Brick. If any divorcing has to be done, he would be the one to decide that. Not Hazel, and not anybody else. He licked his lips and hissed, "You are an ungrateful disagreeable woman. What is it that I haven't given you?"

Hazel yawned. "O, Mace, we've been over this before. Not again, please. You are not really married to me, you are married to your work. It's the only thing you are really concerned about, while I—"

"Like to party and dance," Mace interrupted her, while his breathing became loud. "You want to dance around with the cream of the crop, shop around in Paris and London, while I have to work hard in my lab under the light of a harsh desk lamp, bringing in the money."

He took a step closer and shook his finger in Hazel's face. "I thought we had agreed."

"Agreed to what?" Hazel raised her sandy, penciled brows.

"To present ourselves as the perfect couple to the outside world. And then, you'd let me do what I like to do, and I would not object to your crazy antics. Threatening with a divorce is not quite keeping up that picture to the outside world. "

A shadow that indicated her patience was low, flashed over Hazel's face. "There's only so much pretending a woman can do, Mace. I've done my part. Everybody likes us, but *I* no longer like you. I am sick and tired of your grumpy, stressed-out face, your stupid research, and your constant complaints about other people. You never—"

"Hush, woman," Mace stopped her. "There's a long list of *nevers* that I can hold against you, but if you want to continue this nonsense, I'll tell you, I am prepared."

Hazel leaned back. "What do you mean?"

Mace grinned. "If you run off like that, you will not get *one* cent from me. You will be as poor as the lady cleaning toilets on First Avenue." Hazel's face dropped. The plastic smile she put on, that time when she had paraded on the cover of Vogue Magazine, was nowhere in sight; rather her face resembled that of a beaten warthog who was about to be served as lunch by a group of angry natives. "W-Why?" she stammered.

Mace shook his head. Did Hazel really think he was so dumb as to let her run off with his money? "The day we married, my lawyers drew up a special clause, just for cases like this. It's legal, dear… As long as I am alive I would advise you to stick it out."

Hazel's lip began to tremble and her face slid back into that natural pout of hers that she so often manifested behind closed doors. How he disliked that look.

"I-I just wanted to get your attention, Mace," she mumbled at last. "I am not serious."

"I thought so," Mace said. He had been to this rodeo before. What did she think?

Hazel put her nail polish down on the nightstand and walked towards the cupboard. Mace followed her with his eyes. Were those tears in her eyes?

Hazel opened the oak sliding door of the clothing cupboard and rummaged around for something. At last she pulled out her Shahtoosh shawl and dabbed her eyes with it.

Mace wrinkled his nose. He had seen right. She was crying. Typical Hazel. What woman wipes her tears off with a $5000 shawl?

"Why did you bring that stupid scarf anyway?" he said when it appeared Hazel had finally gotten ahold of herself again. "We are on a cruise ship for crying out loud. Here you don't need a scarf."

"This is not a scarf," she bit back, "this is a shawl, and just for your information, so you won't appear to be ignorant, it's a Shahtoosh shawl. But you don't understand such things. I told you before it's handmade and woven with the down hair of the Tibetan antelope. It's not to ward against the cold, it's for looks."

Mace shook his head. He did not need the hair of an antelope. What he needed were the wings of a dove, so he could fly away to his research-lab and be at peace. But now he had to deal with an increasing amount of silly difficulties.

"Let's go to dinner," he said at last. "So we appear to be the perfect couple that we are, so my son Geoffrey will have a good time."

"You'll have to wait," Hazel murmured. "You've messed up my makeup, and I need to powder my nose again."

Mace looked up to the ceiling and sighed with exasperation. When would this never-ending story finally stop?

When Molly Gertrude and Dora entered the spacious dining area with its wide windows that offered a most splendid view of the ocean, most of the guests had already arrived. The place was filled with the happy chatter and laughter so common to a group of people with hungry stomachs who were in eager anticipation of a wonderful meal. As the two friends stepped onto the soft, plush carpet on the floor they marveled, as a splendid scene enfolded before their eyes. A five star restaurant would not have looked any better. The main dining table was richly decorated, complete with elegant flowers artfully arranged in delicate, hand painted vases, and silver candelabra's. The iconic flowery Wedgwood-design of the serving dishes with the side plates would make eating here a culinary experience that neither Molly Gertrude nor Dora had ever experienced, not even in their wildest dreams. Napkins, exquisitely folded, were placed right next to shiny, engraved crystal wine goblets that sparkled in the light and seemed to cry out to be filled and then emptied into the mouths of whoever would touch them. Molly Gertrude and Dora hardly ever drank a glass of wine, but when Dora saw what was before her, she couldn't help but lick her lips and whisper, "Wine is good for seasickness too. That's what Hampus Rosenqvist told me."

"He did, huh?" Molly Gertrude arched her brows. "Don't believe everything he tells you," she whispered back, but she too decided she would have to at least sample whatever it was the crew would serve in those goblets, as she had never before felt the touch of genuine crystal to her lips.

Molly Gertrude couldn't help but wonder what would happen to all that beauty in the event of a typhoon, but Dora gave her little chance to think such thoughts as she exclaimed, "We are blessed, Miss Molly Gertrude. Truly blessed."

As Molly Gertrude beheld the splendor before her, she couldn't help but wonder why she had even been hired in the first place. It appeared Hazel Brick was quite capable of organizing the event herself. Even though there were other guests on the ship, people that had not been invited to the wedding, Hazel had demanded that for the duration of the cruise, the main dining area on the El Vivo would be reserved only for the wedding guests. The others were directed to a small dining area on the far end of the upper deck, still nice, still gorgeous, but nothing like the dining area Hazel Brick had prepared for the wedding guests.

To foster a spirit of camaraderie she had ordered the dining tables to be placed all together in a broken circle. "That way," Hazel said, "we are all close together during mealtime for this monumental month at sea." Name cards had been carefully and strategically placed on the snow white table linen and, also at Hazel's request, these tags would be switched around every meal, thus forcing everyone to mingle in hopes of creating a happy, joyful atmosphere.

A quick scan of the place told Molly Gertrude the Bricks themselves had not yet arrived. However they did spot a young fellow, dressed in a Hawaiian shirt who was cuddling up to a shy looking girl with long blond hair. Like the dress Molly Gertrude had seen on Hazel earlier, she too wore a sleeveless beach dress. Would that be Geoffrey Brick and his wife-to-be, Evelyn? It almost had to be. The young man did indeed have some of the same facial features as Mace Brick, but his eyes were much softer. He seemed not nearly as hard as his father Mace. And the girl, although dressed like Hazel, radiated a certain softness as well.

Molly Gertrude liked them. Maybe Mace Brick was as hard as a rock, and his wife as proud as a peacock, but for the sake of these two young people it was important to make this wedding a success.

Dora only had eyes on the table that was spread out before them. She rubbed her hands together, stuck her nose in the air to smell the delicious scents that wafted from Hampus Rosenqvist's kitchen, and urged Molly Gertrude forward. "Let's find our name cards, Miss Molly Gertrude, so we can sit down." Without waiting for Molly Gertrude's reply she stepped forward and began to read the cards at the empty spots at the table.

Molly spotted Dr. Biddle. The man had just unfolded his napkin and was tying it around his neck. When he saw Dora and Molly Gertrude reading the name cards he gave her a forced smile. Molly Gertrude cringed. Hopefully she did not need to sit right next to him. But her fears were unfounded. The card before the empty seat by his side read something like Cornelia something… She couldn't quite read it, but in any case, it wasn't Molly Gertrude's name. Molly Gertrude passed by Guillermo DaCosta as well. The seats on his left were still empty as well, but those seats weren’t reserved for them either. The card read Hazel Brick.

Guillermo didn't look at her, or maybe he acted as if he had not seen her. He was still wearing his flip-flops and made small talk with a pretty lady in a pink evening gown who sat on the opposite side of the table.

"Can't seem to find our place," Dora murmured to Molly Gertrude.

She was right. Their names were not on the table,

and before long they were back at their starting point.

A tall waiter, a fellow with a bristly moustache and beady eyes stood nearby with folded arms. Molly Gertrude waddled over to him and asked him for help. But the man gave them an empty stare and answered in a genteel voice, "Your names? They are not here." He glanced down at them in a way that made Molly Gertrude feel she was just about four years old, while she guessed she could be this fellow's grandma.

"Why not?"

The man shrugged his shoulders that were covered by his carefully starched waiter's uniform. "Because you don't belong here. That's why."

"Excuse me?" Dora gasped who by now had joined Molly Gertrude. "Of course we do."

"Of course you don't," the man replied in sharp tones. "Aren't you the hired wedding planners?"

"Yes," Molly Gertrude sneered. "At least, you got that right."

"That explains it," the waiter said. "You are not one of the invited guests. You can get a plate in the kitchen."

"What do you mean?"

"You did not pay for this cruise, so you can't sit at the table either."

"But none of these guests paid for it," Dora complained.

The man did not give an inch. "You are not part of the inner circle. Sorry. I did not make the rules. This is just the way it is."

For a moment Molly Gertrude considered what the effect would be if she gave that arrogant. fellow with his condescending smile, a good hard push in his belly, but as soon as she thought about it, she rebuked that unwelcome thought. Such a thought could not have been inspired by God. Thus, she forced a smile on her face, and said in a meek voice. "Thank you, sir. You've been most helpful. Come Dora, we have to eat elsewhere."

Dora grunted but followed Molly Gertrude. Molly Gertrude did not step into the kitchen but walked out again towards the deck. " Sorry, Dora," she said. "I just need a bit of fresh air."

"This cruise sure holds a few surprises for us, isn't that so, Miss Molly Gertrude?" Dora asked as they stood at the railing.

"It sure seems like it," Molly Gertrude replied, "but have you seen the bride and groom? For their sake, we will do the very best we can."

And so the two friends stood side by side staring over the ocean. It was a blessed moment as the salty sea air, and the cool, refreshing wind that blew through their hair helped to calm them down. Right when Molly Gertrude was about to go back inside, to the kitchen, to ask for a plate of food they heard a woman's voice; angry, irritated and sharp.

"You make my blood boil..."

Molly Gertrude glanced at Dora. "Did you hear that?" she asked. Dora nodded. She had heard the same thing.

Then there was more of the same. "You are a liar, you always have been," the voice continued, now quite agitated.

"Please Cornelia, let's not push our point." Another voice seemed to want to calm down the other person. This was a male voice and it came from very close by. Just on the other side of the lifeboats where the people were arguing.

"Let's find out what's going on," Molly Gertrude whispered. She placed her finger to her lips and motioned with her head for Dora to follow her. Without further ado, she moved as stealthily towards the lifeboat as her old legs would carry her. Dora followed. Now they could hear the conversation better.

"Nonsense," they heard another voice say. This one was male too and it sounded somewhat familiar. "You are nothing but a leech."

Molly Gertrude moved closer to the edge of the lifeboat, careful so as to not make any noise or to get her foot stuck in a rope that was lying around. Once there she peered around the boat ever so carefully. A small shock coursed through her body. Hazel and Mace Brick were arguing with another couple that Molly Gertrude had never seen. The woman was about the same age as Mace. Her messy, long blond curls were fluttering in the wind and she stared at Mace and Hazel with tightened fists. The male beside her, possibly her husband, seemed nervous and tried to calm her down. "I said, let's leave it at this, Cornelia." He seemed ill at ease and clearly wanted this conversation to be over. But the woman called Cornelia shook her head, which caused her curls to fly around even more. "I'll get you, Mace Brick," she hissed. "I won't be satisfied until I see you dead and buried."

Molly Gertrude shivered. That was a horrible thing to say.

"I am expected at dinner," Mace growled. "I have no time for this nonsense. Come Hazel, we've got more important issues to deal with." After he said it, he turned around, grabbed Hazel's hand and dragged her to the dining room, leaving the bewildered couple behind. Molly Gertrude snuck back to where Dora was standing.

"What was that all about?" Dora whispered.

"I don't know," Molly Gertrude whispered back, "but it sure seems Mace Brick is not the popular fellow he claims to be."

A few seconds later, the other couple followed Mace and Hazel and went inside the dining area as well, leaving Molly Gertrude and Dora alone on the deck. "What now?" Dora asked.

"What do you think," Molly Gertrude said with a twinkle in her eye. "The kitchen. I could eat a horse… a small one," she corrected herself. "That waiter told us to go to the kitchen for a plate of food."

Dora's eyes lit up. "I am hungry too, and maybe I'll

introduce you to Hampus. You'll like him," Dora giggled. "He's nice. Almost as nice as Digby."

As they stepped back inside they heard music and singing. It was the voice of Carlos Manual Ureña. He was apparently providing the live music during dinner. They heard his well-trained voice echoing throughout the dining room while they made their way to the kitchen. He sang the same song he had been singing while the El Vivo was still in the harbor. The guests seemed to like it and were gently swaying along on the rhythm. But to Molly Gertrude it became more and more clear that something on this ship was terribly off.

Mi sol tu eres mi sol en mi vida
Quiero dar mi vida por ti

CHAPTER SIX

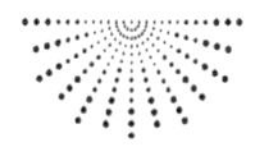

3 **days out...**

Molly Gertrude awoke with a headache. The mattress on the bottom bunk had been rather uncomfortable, Dora had been snoring, and that coupled with the incessant roar in the engine room had made for a rather unpleasant couple of nights. She stretched out one more time, but then, and with great difficulty, swung her old legs over the edge of the bed and forced herself out.

The top bunk was empty.

"Dora?" Molly Gertrude called out. "Are you here?"

As Molly Gertrude was saying it, she knew it was a rather useless question. The cabin was so small that there was no room to hide anywhere and the door to the lavatory was open. But then, right when Molly Gertrude was pondering whether or not it was a good idea to try one of those pills against seasickness in an effort to battle her headache, the door to the cabin opened and Dora appeared. She was very pale, and her eyes were round and wide.

"Morning, Dora," Molly Gertrude mumbled. "Are you seasick again? I have still got these pills." She offered her the strip, but Dora pushed them away. "Murder, Miss Molly Gertrude. There's been a murder."

For a fraction of a second, Molly Gertrude stared at Dora, and her mouth fell open. But then she regrouped her senses, narrowed her eyes and asked in a firm voice, "Who? What? Where?"

All at once she no longer felt her throbbing head, and all the discomfort of the cabin was gone.

"I was hungry," Dora stammered. "You were still snoring, so I snuck out and went to the kitchen. But when I got to the middle deck I was met with terrible confusion."

"What did you see?"

"People running around crying. I spotted Hazel Brick too. She was sitting on a stool, as white as a sheet. Somebody, one of the guests, a strange fellow in flip-flops, was serving her a glass of water, and kept on patting her back as if he wanted to comfort her."

"Guillermo DaCosta," Molly Gertrude mumbled. "I met him yesterday."

"Captain Coakes was there too, and he was telling everyone to be calm, but when I asked him what was going on he told me to just go down to my cabin and stay put for now."

"And then?"

"I saw the engineer that we met yesterday; Bax or Wax, I can't remember his name, he was there too…"

"Dax," Molly Gertrude helped out. "Did he say something?"

"He did," Dora said. "I asked him what was going on. At first he did not seem to even hear me. I guess he was in some sort of a shock. But then, when I kept on pestering him about it, he finally told me what had happened. Mace Brick is dead. He was murdered last night."

Molly Gertrude's eyes became as wide as Dora's. "Mace Brick, the father of the groom is dead?"

"As a doornail," Dora added. "Someone strangled him in his cabin with a scarf or something."

Dora wanted to say more, but they were interrupted by a loud knock on the door. "Miss Grey?" came a demanding male voice. "Open up. I need to talk to you."

Molly Gertrude, hesitated, but Dora urged her on. "Open up, Miss Molly Gertrude. I believe it is the voice of Captain Coakes."

Dora was right.

A second later the captain stood in front of them. His nose was twitching and he constantly turned the wedding ring on his ring finger around. While he had seemed so together yesterday, he now appeared more like a little boy standing in front of the headmistress of primary school, hoping he would be allowed to go home to see his mother. "Miss Grey," he began "I need to ask you a favor."

"Ask," Molly Gertrude replied, not sure how to behave; as the man, although acting so insecure, was fully dressed in his stately uniform, while she was standing before him in her shabby nightgown with a red and green butterfly print.

"We've got a situation," Captain Coakes continued. "A

man has been found dead, and we believe he was murdered."

Molly Gertrude nodded. "Dora just told me, Captain."

"We are miles away from civilization, and it might be days before we can get assistance from the authorities. In the meantime we have a killer on board the El Vivo."

"I understand," Molly Gertrude remarked while squeezing her chin. "What can I do about it?"

Captain Coakes pressed his lips together. "You've got quite a reputation, Miss Grey. Would you be willing to start the murder investigation? It would calm down the nerves of all the guests on board this vessel…" He hesitated and then said, "…the one thing we do not need right now is a panic."

Molly Gertrude sucked in her lips and thought for a moment. Then she looked at Dora. Her co-worker still stared at her with these round, wide eyes. "What do you think, Dora?" Molly Gertrude asked.

"You-uh…I," Dora was still in a state of shock. "Y-You decide, Miss Molly Gertrude."

Molly Gertrude nodded and then turned her attention back to Captain Coakes. "Of course,

Captain," she said. "I will do my best. Just let me get dressed and we'll come as soon as we can."

"Of course," Captain Coakes replied respectfully. "Come to Mace Brick's cabin as soon as you can. My engineer, Dax, will be waiting outside your door, and he'll bring you to Brick's cabin."

Minutes later Dax accompanied Molly Gertrude and Dora to the upper deck.

"Would you mind getting us a cup of raspberry tea and a few sandwiches," Molly Gertrude asked the engineer when they stepped out of the elevator and passed by the main restaurant. "I really need to eat something. My mind does not seem to work when my stomach is empty."

Dax nodded and motioned for one of the waiters. Molly Gertrude recognized the man. It was the same waiter who had directed them so haughtily to the kitchen several days before. "Amram…," the engineer commanded, "Get breakfast ready for these two ladies."

The man arched his brows. "Breakfast?"

"You heard me, man," Dax fired back. "Get them a

plate from the buffet. Captain's orders and hurry up. These ladies are in charge of the murder investigation."

The waiter ran off and Dora couldn't help but suppress a grin. "Murder is always bad," she whispered, "but it has its good sides."

Molly Gertrude blushed. She said nothing but hoped Dax had not heard Dora's off-beat comment.

"Did you know Mr. Brick well?" Molly Gertrude asked Dax a minute later when they sat at the round table with a plate of buns, eggs, a cup of steaming hot tea and other goodies. "I may as well begin my investigation right here."

Dax stiffened. "Not so well," he said. "I know he was a scientist. I read some of his publications."

"You did? What was the man researching?"

"Dark matter."

"What's that?" Molly Gertrude asked while she dipped part of a bun in her tea.

Dax shrugged his shoulders. "It's non-luminous material that is postulated to exist in space and it can take several forms. Sometimes it includes weakly interacting particles."

Both Dora and Molly Gertrude stared at Dax, clearly not understanding the man. Dax noticed, and he grinned, "You asked, so I answered, but I dare say, for your murder investigation it is of no consequence."

"You seem to know a lot about it," Molly Gertrude replied while she studied the engineer. "That's not the kind of knowledge you'd expect from the first engineer on a cruise-ship."

Dax offered Molly Gertrude a sheepish smile. "I told you before I did a bit of dabbling in scientific theories."

"Right," Molly Gertrude said. She took a sip from her tea and then asked, "You told me yesterday the man was rude and that his mother had not done a very good job. Why did you say such a thing?"

Dax wrinkled his nose and shifted position. "Why are you asking me such questions? Am I a suspect too?"

Molly Gertrude smiled. "Of course not, Dax. I am just trying to get the picture straight. Every person here on this boat has a part of the puzzle. You are just the first one I came in contact with."

Dax nodded, apparently satisfied with Molly

Gertrude's answer. He moved his beanie a little tighter over his forehead and said, "Just ask anyone here. Everyone agrees. The man is dishonest and—"

"Why?"

"I don't know," Dax replied. "He just is."

Molly frowned, but said nothing. She finished her bun and said. "Thank you Dax. That's all for now. If you don't mind leading us now to Mr. Brick's cabin, I can start my investigation."

"Already?" Dora said. She looked disappointed as she had several pieces of breakfast cake on her plate. She had just finished a hefty serving of eggs and sausage and 2 slices of fluffy French toast were begging her to be eaten, in addition to the cake. Molly Gertrude however was not in the mood to put pleasure before work and shook her head. "You can eat all you want later, Dora. We just needed to get something in our tummies. Dora sighed and pushed the dish aside, got up, and mumbled an apology.

Minutes later they stood before Mace Brick's cabin. An officer stood nearby and was apparently guarding the place. "Miss Grey?" he asked while looking at Molly Gertrude. "I am Chief Mate Harrison. The Captain is back on the bridge, but he asked me to stay here for now, and guard the place until you have looked around and afterwards we can clean the place up."

"Who found the body?" Molly Gertrude asked.

"I believe it was Mrs. Bricks herself. You'll have to ask her yourself."

Molly Gertrude nodded, and opened the door. Mace Brick lay on the floor, his arms outstretched. His face had a strange, unnatural color. When Molly stepped inside to take a better look, someone tried to brush by, but bumped into her in the process. "What…?"

It was Dr. Rasheed Biddle.

"Dr. Biddle?" Molly Gertrude exclaimed.

When the doctor saw Molly his face turned red. "W-Why are you here?" he mumbled.

"I am in charge of the investigation until we can get the real police involved," Molly Gertrude answered. "But why are *you* here?"

"I-I've got nothing to do with the crime," he said. His voice was hoarse and strained. "I know what I told you yesterday, but of course, eh… I didn't really mean that."

"You *did* tell me you wanted both Hazel and Mace

Brick out of your life," Molly Gertrude said. "And you also said you had made preparations." Molly tilted her head. "What were you talking about?"

"A good lawyer," Dr. Biddle fired back. "That's all. It's true, I didn't like Mace, but I am not a murderer. I am a doctor who swore the Hippocratic Oath. I save lives, I do not take it."

Molly Gertrude studied the man, who seemed so eager to leave. "You still haven't answered my question," she asked at last. "What are you doing here?"

"It's *obvious* what I am doing," Biddle grunted. "I am the Brick's family doctor, and the only doctor on board of this vessel. It's my job to be here."

"I suppose it is," Molly Gertrude answered. "And what did you find?"

"Not much," the man shrugged. "It is my guess, he was strangled with that scarf. The marks on his neck confirm it." He pointed to an expensive looking shawl that was placed on the floor, right next to the dead man's body. "It is Hazel's shawl. She always wears it on special occasions."

"Was that shawl on the floor?"

The doctor shook his head. "I found it in the garbage

container. But a shawl like this costs about $5,000. I don't think Hazel would have carelessly dumped it in the trash." He walked over to the bed and picked up the shawl. "There's blood on it too, just like there's blood on his strangled neck." He showed it to Molly Gertrude who studied it and gave the man a nod. It made sense

"Can you tell how long the man has been dead?"

Dr. Biddle clucked his tongue. "It's hard to tell. Judging by the looks and the stiffness of his body, I imagine he died somewhere between ten and twelve last night."

"And where were you at that hour?"

"Me?" Rasheed Biddle grinned. "I was dancing and drinking in the dining area. Ask Amram. He's the head waiter, and he'll tell you about my night."

"Amram?" Molly Gertrude asked. "That tall fellow with the bristly moustache?"

"Yeah," Dr. Biddle replied. "Amram Boletti. He's a friendly fellow."

Molly Gertrude pondered the doctor's alibi. Biddle had been rather outspoken about his dislike for Mace Brick, and since there were no other medical personnel around to verify Biddle's findings, the man could easily fake the time of death. She needed to keep an eye on this man.

"Thank you, Doctor," she said at last. "You didn't find anything else?"

"No," he stated simply. "What else could there be? Can I go now?"

"Sure," Molly Gertrude said. "If I need some more information, I will find you."

Biddle got up and left the spacious cabin without saying another word.

"So what do you think so far, Miss Molly Gertrude?" Dora asked, while filling up on a bag of raisins the Swedish Chef, Hampus Rosenqvist, had given her the night before. "It's too early to tell," Molly Gertrude replied, "Right now, we know very little."

After they had looked around in the cabin of the Bricks, and had not found any other visible clues, they stepped out again, smiled at First Mate Harrison and were now on their way to Captain Coakes on the bridge.

"First of all, we need to ask the Captain for a list of

all the passengers. And I suppose, we need to talk to that couple we overheard two nights ago, those folks behind the lifeboat. They sure did not sound like friends of Mace Brick's."

"Right," Dora said. "And what about Hazel Brick herself?"

Molly nodded. "She claimed she found her husband's body. We need to talk to her as well. Her husband was killed with her shawl. Then there is Rasheed Biddle, that fellow we just bumped into. He personally told me he hated both, Hazel and Mace."

"So do a lot of other people," Dora said with a sigh. "That Dax fellow was pretty outspoken too." As they climbed up to the bridge, another thought hit Dora. "And what about the bride? Didn't Dr. Biddle tell you the Bricks forced her to sign some sort of legal document that would ensure she would be pretty much under the control of the Bricks for the rest of her life?"

"He did...," Molly Gertrude replied while thinking about it, "...and I suppose we need to keep that in mind. But I studied that girl yesterday at the dinner table. I don't think she is the type to commit a murder, neither does she have the strength for it."

"Couldn't she have hired someone to do it?"

"Anything is possible," Molly Gertrude said. "But I doubt it. My hunches about people are usually right, and I don't think that girl has anything to do with it."

Dora blew out a long puff of air. "And now we are only talking about the people we *do* know about," she mumbled. "Only God knows how many people there are involved that we do *not* yet know about." But then she turned to Molly Gertrude and chuckled, "In any case, cheer up, Miss Molly Gertrude. You told me yourself you were bored. So look at this… what a good thing it was that we embarked on this adventure."

Molly Gertrude turned to Dora and gave her a warm smile. "You sure are right about that, Dora. We've got our work cut out for us."

They had arrived at the bridge.

CHAPTER SEVEN

"What a terrible, *terrible* event," Hazel Brick moaned while she stared with teary eyes at Molly Gertrude and Dora from her deckchair. "But," she added, "you two are wasting your time. I am not in the mood to talk about the wedding."

The two friends had walked up to her, and asked to talk to her. "We do not want to discuss the wedding, Mrs. Brick," Molly Gertrude clarified. "We would like to talk to you about your husband."

As soon as the word husband had left Molly Gertrude's mouth, Hazel broke out into a hysterical wail. "Oh my poor, poor husband," she cried out. "We were such a good team and we loved each other through thick and thin." She leaned forward, grabbed the cocktail right next to her on a small side table, and took a sip. "It helps me to forget," she explained, while she stared with big, watery eyes at Molly Gertrude and Dora. "What is it you want to know about my husband? To be honest, I'd rather be alone right now."

Molly Gertrude cleared her throat. "Captain Coakes has asked me to look into the murder, since there's no police presence yet."

Hazel Brick's demeanor changed, and her eyes switched back to their original hardness. "You two are investigating?" she mumbled in disbelief.

"I am afraid so," Molly Gertrude said. "Do you mind?"

"Of course I mind," Hazel fired back, "but I guess I have no choice, do I?"

Molly Gertrude chose not to react to Hazel's statement. Instead she asked a question she knew would likely cause more sparks to fly. "Did you love each other?"

"Of course we did," Hazel fumed. "What kind of a question is that during the period of my mourning?"

"I do not mean to be offensive," Molly Gertrude spoke in a gentle tone, "but I have witnesses that told me you and Mr. Brick weren't as tight as you wanted the world to believe."

Hazel Brick flew into a rage, almost knocking off her cocktail from the side table. "We were just about as close as can be expected in this dog-eat-dog society," she hissed. "I want my lawyer here."

"He's not here," Molly Gertrude stated, "and this talk is not official since I am not a police officer, but we talked to Rasheed Biddle, and he told us you were thinking of a divorce—"

"—He said that?" Hazel howled. "That man knows nothing. He's as incompetent in the medical field as a rabbit in a chemistry lab. Now that Mace is gone, I'll fire him today."

"You do what you like," Molly Gertrude replied a little stiffly, "but he also said that Mace had a legal document drawn up, that stated you would not get anything in case of a divorce…"

Hazel's jaws tightened and her hand went back to her cocktail.

"But…," Molly continued, "…it appears since Mace died, you inherit everything."

"So?" Hazel gritted her teeth and stared defiantly at

Molly Gertrude and Dora. "That doesn't mean I killed him."

"No, it doesn't," Molly Gertrude agreed, "but it did give you a motive." Hazel's face was now bright red, and it had nothing to do with the sun. Molly Gertrude could tell she was making an enemy. Thank God, Mace had made a down payment for the wedding arrangements before they had left Calmhaven.

"You two are fired," Hazel rasped. "I don't need your help with the wedding anymore."

"I understand," Molly Gertrude said in a calm voice. "But as I said, I am not here to discuss the wedding. Tell me, when did you actually find your husband?"

"Early this morning," Hazel said in icy tones.

"When?"

"At four in the morning. I entered the cabin and there he was, all sprawled out on the floor."

"And where were you before you found him?"

"In the private swimming pool," Hazel fired back. "I go there to be alone, away from stupid people like you."

Molly Gertrude let Hazel's sting roll off like water

on a duck's back. "I am sorry to have to do this, Mrs. Brick. But it's my job right now." She paused for a moment, and then said, "So… can somebody testify you were at the swimming pool until four o'clock?"

"Nobody," Hazel grunted, "That's why I go to the pool, because it is private, but I did not kill my husband."

Molly Gertrude nodded. "Anything else you can remember about last night?"

Hazel pressed her lips together. "Nothing, besides the fact that the air conditioner, in the pool area, didn't seem to be working. It blew out cold air instead of hot air. Dax will have to fix that."

At that moment someone passed by. Hazel's face became softer and she sat up again. "Mr. DaCosta," she cried out, "Can you tell me what time it is?"

Molly Gertrude turned around and stared in the face of the charming Guillermo DaCosta. But this time he was not smiling. He was still wearing his flip-flops, but rather looked like a kid that was caught with his hands in a cookie jar. "Hello, Miss Grey," he mumbled in an uncertain way. Then he pulled his sleeve back, and answered Hazel Brick's question. "It's ten past one, Mrs. Brick."

"Thank you, Mr. DaCosta," Hazel said with a satisfied grin. She turned to Molly Gertrude and snorted, "In that case, you will have to excuse me, Miss Grey. I've got an appointment that I cannot possibly miss, and since you are not the official police, you can't stop me. Bye, bye."

Molly Gertrude shook her head. The depth of this woman's arrogance seemed bottomless. "Sure, Mrs. Brick. We won't keep you from your important meeting on a day like this."

"Good," Hazel replied. She stretched herself out on the deck chair and without even looking at Molly Gertrude and Dora she waved them away with her hand and sneered again, "Goodbye."

"Phew," Dora blurted out when they were out of sight of Hazel Brick. "She is quite a lady. You stayed so calm, Miss Molly Gertrude. I felt like shaking her around a few times."

"I did too, Dora," Molly Gertrude chuckled, "but that's not quite the behavior you would expect of an old lady, is it?"

"I guess not," Dora said with a grin, "but she is

definitely on the black list. She's a liar, she has a motive, and no alibi."

"Still, it is too early to jump to a conclusion," Molly Gertrude said. She had been in the sleuthing business long enough to know that things are not always what they seem to be. Molly Gertrude wanted to say something more, but as they were walking towards the elevator, she was interrupted by a soft voice on the side.

"Pssst, over here," the voice said.

Molly Gertrude stopped and turned. There was the woman with the messy, long blond curls who had been arguing two days before with Mace and Hazel Brick. "H-Hello," Molly Gertrude said, and arched her brow. "What can we do for you?"

Now that Molly Gertrude wasn't hiding behind a lifeboat, she could take a better look at the woman. In some ways she resembled Hazel. She had a bit of the same mannerism and style, except that she was quite a bit older, and apparently had stopped caring for her waist-line as she was a bit on the heavy side. The woman sat on a large bench that, like all benches on the ship, gave a beautiful view over the ocean.

"Aren't you Miss Grey, the one in charge of the murder investigation?" she began.

"That's right," Molly Gertrude replied.

"Sit with me. I'd like to talk to you," the lady said with a grand, inviting smile, and patted the empty space on the bench beside her.

"My name is Cornelia Callmedt," the lady said. "My husband Harry is the CEO of Callmedt Incorporated. I am sure you must have heard the name."

Molly Gertrude had not, and neither had Dora, thus they stared blankly at Mrs. Callmedt.

"Never mind," Cornelia sang. "It's a small company. We are dealing in toothpaste, you know."

"Interesting," Molly Gertrude said, not wanting to appear rude.

"I'll get you some samples," Cornelia went on. "If you'd like of course."

"That's very kind of you," Molly Gertrude said politely, " but right now my assistant and I are rather busy, so why don't you come to the point. What is it you would like to discuss with us?"

"Oh, of course, I am sorry," Cornelia mumbled. She

licked off some of her bright red lipstick, and then said in a conspiratorial voice while leaning forward, "It's about Hazel Brick."

"Really?" Molly Gertrude said. "What about her?"

Cornelia looked around as if to make sure no one could overhear and then said, "Hazel Brick is a duplicitous and untrustworthy character."

"Really?"

Cornelia nodded. "She sure is, and she is capable of any depth of betrayal. I wouldn't be surprised if she's the one that killed Mace Brick."

"What makes you say such a thing?" Molly Gertrude asked.

Cornelia seemed surprised. "Everybody knows, Miss Grey. It's common knowledge."

"Not to us," Molly Gertrude said.

"Well, you can take my word for it," Cornelia said. "If you ask me, Hazel Brick is only interested in money. Lots of money. She'll deny it of course, but mark my words… she-is-involved."

"Did you perhaps have any personal dealings with the Bricks?" Molly Gertrude asked.

Cornelia turned a little red. "Me? Eh… No. I don't think I have." She shifted her position and then added, "I just want to help, that's all."

Molly Gertrude nodded. "If you really want to help, it would be best if you'd be honest with us, Mrs. Cornbread."

"Callmedt," Cornelia shot back. "My name is Callmedt, and I *am* always honest."

Molly Gertrude's eyes widened. "That's funny. Then why did you say two nights ago, and I quote…" Molly Gertrude paused and fished a notebook out of her bag and read: "… I won't be satisfied until you are dead and buried. You are a liar! You always have been a liar!" Molly Gertrude looked up. "Shall I read more?"

Cornelia turned pale, which made her red-painted lips stand out all the more. "W-Where did you hear that. Who told you?"

"You did," Molly Gertrude said. "You and your husband were arguing with them just before dinner."

"Y-You heard?" Cornelia stared with fearful eyes at Molly Gertrude.

"Yes, we did," Molly Gertrude said.

A tear rolled out of Cornelia's eye. "The Bricks have virtually bankrupted us," she wailed. "They promised us a loan years ago, but they never came through. Thinking we could count on their financial help we made legal commitments for our toothpaste business… It all backfired on us."

"Then why did you say you never had any personal dealings with the Bricks?"

Cornelia stared at Molly Gertrude with sad, drooping eyes. "I was afraid we would be suspects. But you must believe me, my husband and I had nothing to do with the murder. Honestly we didn't."

"Where were you and your husband last night?" Molly Gertrude asked while she stared deep into Cornelia's eyes.

"I did not like the man, but I am not a murderer," Cornelia cried out. "And neither is my husband."

"Then you have nothing to worry about. Just answer my question," Molly Gertrude demanded.

"Last night? Uh…" Cornelia thought long and hard. Then she called out in relief, "I remember." She cast Molly Gertrude an apologetic stare. "I had a bit too much to drink, so I had to refresh my memory. But last night, we were dancing. My husband and I were dancing, all night long. We were dancing to the music of the divine Carlos Manual Ureña." She forced a smile on her face. "You know hits like *One, Two, Three, Love For You And Me*… and *Hold Fast The Dark*.

"Can people confirm that?"

"Of course. Ask the head waiter, Amram Boletti. He's a friendly fellow, and kept on serving us drinks." She giggled. "That's why I had a few too many. Actually, my husband didn't make it to the end of the evening."

"Oh. Why not?"

"He is not much of a drinker," Cornelia giggled some more. "A few beers and he's out. Rasheed dragged him to a bench in the kitchen. He slept there all night."

"Rasheed?"

Cornelia blushed. "I mean Dr. Biddle."

"You know him well?" Molly Gertrude asked.

"Uh…not so much. After my husband passed out, we had a few dances. That's all."

"I see," Molly Gertrude said. Then she glanced at

Dora. "What do you think, Dora? I think we've got all we need for now."

Dora nodded, and Molly Gertrude got up. "Thank you, Mrs. Callmedt. This is it for now."

"Am I no longer a suspect?" Cornelia asked with hopeful eyes.

"We'll talk to Amram Boletti," Molly Gertrude said. "Thank you for your time." She turned to Dora and said, "Come, Dora, we've got to go."

"Did you know..." Cornelia still cried out, but stopped halfway thru her sentence. Molly Gertrude turned her attention back to Cornelia. "Did I know what?"

"Mace Brick forced Evelyn, the bride, to sign a legal document, that virtually puts her at the mercy of the Bricks?"

Molly Gertrude raised her brows. "Yes, I've heard as much," she replied, "But how come you know about it? Wasn't that supposed to be a well-kept secret?"

Cornelia's face turned red again. "I-uh... just heard about it. That's all."

Molly Gertrude studied the woman for a moment. Underneath that mask of so-called helpfulness there seemed to be brewing a world of anger, mistrust and resentment. That woman knew a lot more than she said.

"We'll talk some more," Molly Gertrude said at last. Both friends turned and walked off, leaving a bewildered Cornelia Callmedt behind.

* * *

"What now?" Dora asked. "It seems just about everyone we talk to seems to have a motive for killing Mace Brick. He must have been a rather unpleasant person."

"Still, that's no excuse to murder somebody," Molly Gertrude spoke while she forced her brain to bring some order to the mess of possibilities. But first things first. They needed to at least find out what Amram Boletti had to say, since it appeared everyone used that man as a reference to prove their alibi.

"Would you talk to the head waiter?" Molly Gertrude asked Dora.

"Who, me?" Dora pointed a finger at herself.

"Would you mind?" Molly Gertrude replied. "I am rather tired of having to cross all these decks with my old legs. What's more, I don't think he likes me very much."

"I suppose, that's mutual," Dora said with a grin. "I'll look him up, but if it was up to me, I would just about arrest them all."

Molly Gertrude had to laugh. "I suppose we should be thankful that you are not in charge, Dora Brightside. That would be the wrong kind of justice."

"Whatever," Dora groused. "But that's how I feel."

"What do you think about Guillermo DaCosta?" Molly Gertrude asked.

Dora tilted her head. "You mean that fellow in flip-flops? He seems sort of nice. One of the few."

"Looks can be deceiving," Molly Gertrude retorted. "He's a professional charmer, so he knows how to act. A real womanizer he is, and to be frank, I don't like him."

Dora frowned. "We've already got more suspects than we can handle, Miss Molly Gertrude. Why do you think he's got something to do with it?"

"Because…," Molly Gertrude said, "… I think he's having an affair with Hazel Bricks. Maybe they planned the whole thing together. Hazel gets the money, Guillermo gets the woman... everybody is happy."

Dora's mouth fell open. "You really think so, Miss Molly Gertrude? An illegitimate affair. That sure would be a motive for murder."

"He too has a few secrets," the old sleuth replied with certainty. "What's more, he has a watch."

"A watch?" Dora did not understand. "Most people have a watch. If everyone with a watch is a suspect we would be busy investigating for another year."

"True," Molly Gertrude said, "but yesterday when I first met Guillermo DaCosta, he had *no* watch. And today, Hazel asked him the time, and he *did* have a watch. Where did he get that watch?"

"I don't know," Dora shrugged. "Maybe he bought one in the duty-free shop."

Molly Gertrude nodded. "That's possible. But *what* if he murdered Brick and took his watch. Mace Brick was such a snob, he must have been walking around with a diamond studded watch. Stealing such a watch would be a motive in itself. It wouldn't be difficult to confront Guillermo DaCosta with this theory."

Dora licked her lips as she thought about Molly

Gertrude's theory. "Or...," she added, "... to stay in line with your idea..., what if Hazel *gave* him the watch, after he killed Mace? Sort of like the dividing of the spoils."

"Good thinking, Dora," Molly Gertrude said. "As I always say, it's all in the details." She thought for a moment and then asked, "And Biddle, what do you think of him? He sure hated Mace Brick."

Dora shrugged her shoulders. "I don't know, Miss Molly Gertrude. As I said, so many people disliked Mr. Brick. Maybe we should first talk to Guillermo DaCosta." Her eyes sparkled. "My hunch is that it's him."

"Not yet," Molly Gertrude shook her head. "I would first like to talk to Geoffrey Brick."

Dora narrowed her eyes. "The son? Surely, you don't think he killed his own father?"

"Probably not," Molly Gertrude said, "but we can't exclude him, Dora. Maybe he found out about his father having forced his sweetheart into signing that horrible deal. I don't think he did it, but he may know details that will help us to find out what really happened. It's important we talk to him."

"As you wish, Miss Molly Gertrude," Dora said. "You

always have a better sense than I do. You want to do that now?"

Molly Gertrude nodded. "You talk to Amram, and I'll see if I can find Geoffrey Brick. That is the one good thing about a murder at sea. Nobody can get away, including the murderer, so he or she is still among us."

CHAPTER EIGHT

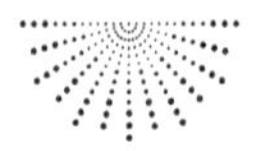

Geoffrey appeared genuinely broken about his father's passing. Molly Gertrude found him in the lounge, alone and confused. His wife-to-be, Evelyn, apparently had a headache and was resting in her cabin.

When Molly Gertrude asked him if she could talk to him about his dad, he looked up with a tear-stained face. "Of course," he said. "Excuse me for my tears. My father was not much loved, but he still was my father, and I just don't understand why anyone would do such a horrible thing."

"Neither do I," Molly Gertrude said. "Sadly, we live in a broken world. It never ceases to amaze me to what length some people will go to get their way. I am very sorry for your loss."

"Thank you," Geoffrey said. "What would you like to know?"

"Captain Coakes has asked me to investigate this murder, which is why I am here."

Geoffrey pressed his lips together and gave her a sad nod. Molly studied the young man sitting at the table before her. Traces of his boyhood were still visible, but he was not a boy anymore. He wore a simple red T-shirt but his arms were muscled and strong. He probably spent a lot of time at the gym. His boyish smile came easy, even in a trying time like this, and as Molly Gertrude stared into his innocent green eyes, she found it hard to believe this young man would be capable of committing such a horrendous crime. Still, looks could be deceiving.

"How was your relationship with your father?" she asked.

Without hesitation, Geoffrey replied, "My father was not a nice man. I dare say he was a tyrant, and he had many enemies."

"Did he like… uh, Evelyn, your wife-to-be?"

Geoffrey shook his head. "No, he did not." He paused for a moment and then added, "You may find this hard to believe, Miss Grey, but in spite of the fact that virtually all his acquaintances hated him, I *did* really love him."

"And your mother. Did she love your father?"

"Which one?"

His answer puzzled Molly Gertrude. "I mean Hazel Brick. I know your father married twice before, but I just figured Hazel is your mother."

He shook his head and couldn't suppress a grin, although it appeared to be a bit sour. "Don't you think Hazel would be a bit young to be my mother, Miss Grey? But to be clear, Hazel is not my mother. And to be perfectly honest, Hazel and I have no relationship that is worth mentioning."

Molly Gertrude was not surprised. "Did she love your father?"

Geoffrey shook his head. "Hazel loves money, and since my dad has plenty of it, he was her springboard to wealth. No, I don't think she genuinely loved Dad." After he had said it he gave Molly Gertrude a blank look, and slowly said, "You think Hazel may have killed my dad? That's a terrible accusation." He was silent for a moment and then added, "She was not a good influence on him.

She was, as they say, the neck that turned the head, but murder… I don't know."

Molly Gertrude took it all in. One thing bothered her and at last she decided to just ask. "So if you are not Hazel's son, then where is your real mother? That must have been your dad's second wife."

Geoffrey sighed. "I was not to mention this, but since my father is dead, I suppose it doesn't matter anymore." He gave Molly Gertrude a guilty look.

"I am only asking, so I can better understand the whole situation," Molly Gertrude said, as it seemed Geoffrey was rather uncomfortable with the question.

"She's here," Geoffrey said at last. "On the ship."

Molly Gertrude sat back in her seat. "She is here? Who is it?"

"She has taken on the name of her new husband. Callmedt. Her name is Cornelia Callmedt."

"W-What?" Molly Gertrude blurted out. "You mean *the* Cornelia Callmedt that we just talked to?"

Geoffrey shrugged his shoulders. "I don't know who you just talked to, but as far as I know there's only one Cornelia Callmedt aboard this vessel."

Molly Gertrude rubbed her forehead and blew out a puff of air.

"I wasn't supposed to let anybody know that Cornelia is my real mother," Geoffrey continued. "Both my dad and Hazel didn't want her around on this cruise, but since this was supposed to be my wedding, I insisted my mother be invited." He shook his head and chuckled. "Boy, did we have a fight about that. I don't think I've ever seen Hazel as furious as she was on that day, but I insisted my mom be invited. Dad finally had to buy her a new fur coat to calm Hazel down."

"So your Dad didn't mind?"

"He didn't like it, but he was not as tough as people thought. He had his soft side. Of course, my mom insisted her new husband be invited as well, which complicated matters."

"Why?"

"My Dad was supposed to finance the toothpaste company of my mother's new husband, but he never did. I don't know all the details, but things went sour. I don't think they liked each other very much."

Molly Gertrude looked at the young man in front of her. He seemed to be sandwiched in between a rock and a hard place. There was one other question on Molly Gertrude's lips. A little touchy too. Did he think his real mother, or her new husband were capable of murder?

Geoffrey seemed to guess her thoughts. "Of course, you can question my mother and my step-dad, and you should. But if you ask me, I don't think they had anything to do with it. My mom is even afraid of a spider. She can talk tough, but her heart is as soft as butter."

"Oh?" Molly Gertrude said. "And her husband?"

Geoffrey shook his head. "As far as I can tell he is wimpy. But you'll have to ask him yourself. I came here to get married, not to solve the unexpected murder of my dad."

At that moment Dora entered the lounge. She hesitated when she saw Molly Gertrude and Geoffrey, but Molly Gertrude motioned for her to come and sit.

"Please meet Geoffrey Brick."

Dora sat down and shook hands with the young man. "Sorry for your loss," she said. "My name is Dora Brightside. I am Miss Molly Gertrude's co-worker."

Geoffrey gave her a small, polite smile and looked down at the table.

Molly Gertrude cleared her throat and turned her attention back to Geoffrey.

"Forgive me for asking, Geoffrey," she said, "but just to make sure we do not overlook any of the details…, what were you doing last night?"

"I was dancing," Geoffrey replied without hesitation. "Evelyn and I were dancing all night, until closing time, which was about three in the morning. You can ask the head waiter. His name is—"

"— Amram Boletti," Dora finished his sentence.

Geoffrey looked up in surprise. "Yes. Do you know him?"

"I just came from him," Dora explained. "And he mentioned you and Evelyn were there the whole evening." She turned to Molly Gertrude and added, "And it appears the others were too. It was as they said."

Molly Gertrude squeezed her chin with her fingers. "I see… I see." She narrowed her eyes and asked Geoffrey, "Is there anybody else you think would want to harm your dad?"

"Most of the people on this ship," Geoffrey replied with a sad expression. "I mean, my dad was a well-respected scientist, but as a person he had major flaws." He curled his lips and let out a sneering little laugh. "But dad seemed to enjoy being the man he was.

"How is that?" Molly Gertrude asked.

"He collected each and every article that had anything to do with him. Most people would only collect the favorable articles, but to my Dad, it didn't matter. 'All publicity is good publicity,' he would say and whenever there was an article about him, even a negative one, he would cut it out and glue it in a scrapbook."

"That's strange," Dora said.

"Very strange," Geoffrey admitted. "In fact, I can even show you the book. He always carries it around, and on this trip he keeps it in his cupboard."

Both Dora and Molly Gertrude looked up. "He brought that scrapbook with him on the El Vivo?"

"Yep," Geoffrey said. "He was rather proud of it. Want to see it?"

"Yes," Molly Gertrude replied. "I would like very much to see it."

Geoffrey shrugged his shoulders. "Sure, but it's just a bunch of rubbish."

"Maybe," Molly Gertrude replied, "but I have a hunch that this could be important."

"A hunch?" Geoffrey asked while raising his brows.

"Yes, a hunch," Dora tried to clarify. "Miss Molly Gertrude's hunches are usually right, and they have proven to be very helpful in solving many a crime already. We would really like to see that scrapbook."

"No problem," Geoffrey said, while he glanced at Molly Gertrude with renewed interest. "I've got a key to my father's cabin. Hazel won't be there. I believe she is tanning on the upper deck."

"In that case," Molly Gertrude said, "Let's go."

Not many minutes later, they stood in Mace Brick's cabin again. The body of the dead man was no longer there, as Captain Coakes had ordered it to be taken away. "Just sit," Geoffrey motioned to a sofa, and went to work right away. He opened several drawers, searched around a bit, and then let out a victorious cry. "Got it." He turned to Molly Gertrude with a smile while waving Mace Brick's scrapbook around.

It was a rather bulky book, protected by a red leather cover. Geoffrey handed it to Molly Gertrude. She asked Dora to look with her and they both began to peruse the pages. Mace Brick had been rather meticulous and the scrapbook testified of Mace Brick's organized and scientific approach to a project.

Small articles were all placed on the right pages of the book, while the bigger articles were all on the left. Dates, and pertinent information, such as the reference of the newspaper or magazine, were carefully placed above each individual article in clear and neat handwriting.

As Molly Gertrude turned the pages she shook her head. "Oh my. Mace Brick was indeed quite famous."

"He was," Geoffrey replied. "As you can see, not all the articles are positive, but that didn't matter to my dad. He took great pride in the attention, good or bad."

When Molly Gertrude read the different headlines she realized Geoffrey was right. Some titles were indeed rather flattering, and showed headlines as *The Genius of Brick at work,* or *Brick receives scientific award.* Yet others were not quite so positive. Both Molly Gertrude and Dora cringed when they read headlines like, *Stuff Mace Brick doesn't tell you,* or *Brick sues the homeless.*

Molly Gertrude looked up. "Whatever the world thinks about your dad," she said, "he was undeniably a colorful person."

"You can say that," Geoffrey replied, a little wryly.

One article in particular, it was actually only about six months old, caught Molly Gertrude's attention. It was apparently a rebuttal to an article written by a scientist who had been in opposition to some of Mace Brick's findings about Dark Matter. Molly Gertrude scanned the article and studied the photograph of the scientist that was mentioned in the article.

Mace Brick Wipes Floor with Young Scientist-

By Wilson Crook- New York Times

In a recent publication, well-known scientist Mace Brick has demolished the findings of Maxwell Dubois, the young, rising star in the scientific community. Dubois, who dared to question the validity of Mace Brick's findings on Dark Matter in an article in the American Scientific, last month, has been called by Brick as an incompetent, incapable, immature scientific dwarf, who is as much a scientist as a donkey who had his brain removed.

As I reported some weeks ago, Maxwell Dubois claimed Mace Brick stole the young scientist's data, and claimed them as his own. However, Mace Brick has now sued Dubois for slander and Brick's lawyer claims he has ample proof Dubois is nothing but a derailed scientist who seeks to ride on the coattails of a real professional scientist, who is completely devoted to his cause in his noble efforts to make the earth a better place.

Molly Gertrude looked up at Geoffrey. "This is a rather damning article," she stated. "Did your father ever mention this Maxwell Dubois?

"He sure did," Geoffrey replied. "He hated that man with a perfect hatred, and apparently he got rid of him too."

"What happened?"

"I don't know all the details, and I certainly don't know who is right and who is wrong," Geoffrey replied. "My dad sued Dubois, and won of course." He licked his lips. "It's a matter of money, you know. It seems money talks. But if you want to know more about it, you should ask Hazel." He paused for a moment and then continued. "But that is nothing special. This sort of a thing happened all the time."

Molly Gertrude wanted to ask another question, but right then there was an urgent knock on the door, followed by a distressed voice that cried out in alarm, "Miss Grey? Please, you are needed at the swimming pool."

Geoffrey opened the door and they all stared at First Mate Harrison, his face a mass of fear and misery. "Miss Grey, please... we've got no time to loose. Please follow me to the swimming pool."

"Why, Mr. Harrison?" Molly Gertrude asked.

The First Mate glanced at Geoffrey and seemed hesitant. "I-uh... I'll tell you on the way."

"Tell me now," Molly Gertrude demanded. "What's wrong?"

First Mate Harrison took off his cap, fumbled with it in his hands, and then turned to Geoffrey. "I-I am sorry to be the one to have to tell you this," he said. "But... your mother is dead."

"Dead?" Geoffrey's hand flew up to his forehead. "My mother is dead?"

"I am afraid so," Harrison replied.

But then Geoffrey asked a question that seemed to puzzle First Mate Harrison.

"Which one, Mr. Harrison?" Geoffrey asked.

Harrison scratched his head. "Well-eh... your mother, Mr. Brick. Don't you have only one?"

Geoffrey wrinkled his nose. "Of course, but not everyone knows who my real mother is."

"Hazel Brick," Harrison blurted out. "Isn't she your real mother? It appears she too has been murdered."

As Molly Gertrude and Dora followed First Mate Harrison to the swimming pool countless thoughts raced through Molly Gertrude's head. If Hazel was dead, it was clear she would not have committed the murder of Mace. This changed everything. All suspicion now rested on Guillermo DaCosta. If her hunches were right, and the flip-flop man was having a secret thing going on with Hazel, it was possible he had a secret agenda, and he was nothing more than a common thief and had killed them both for greedy gain.

And what about Cornelia and her new husband? It seemed more and more plausible they had something to do with it…

Molly Gertrude, afflicted by her ever increasing battle with arthritis couldn't keep up with the First Mate and Dora. The two had just rounded a corner and disappeared out of sight, but Molly Gertrude knew where the private pool was situated. She just couldn't go any faster, and Hazel Brick was dead already, so there was no need to hurry.

But then, as she rounded the corner she was in for a surprise. She crashed into someone. It was a man; a hurried man. He came around without looking, seemingly out of nowhere and pushed Molly Gertrude against the wood paneling of a cabin. She rocked and reeled but to her relief she managed to keep her balance. The one who had crashed into her however lay sprawled out before her on the upper deck… Guillermo DaCosta.

"Guillermo," Molly Gertrude cried out. "Can't you watch where you are going?"

"Sorry," Guillermo mumbled as he scraped himself off the floor. "I am in a hurry."

"I can see that," Molly Gertrude spoke in an agitated voice. Guillermo seemed utterly distressed, wiped his forehead, and without saying another word, he ran off again. As Molly Gertrude stared after him, she noticed something strange. The man was not wearing his flip-flops. He was barefoot.

She shrugged her shoulders. Maybe he had forgotten them. In any case, it didn't matter as she needed to hurry to the swimming pool.

The door to the private pool was open. First Mate Harrison and Dora were already inside. As Molly Gertrude stepped through the door she marveled. It was a beautiful pool. Rather small, maybe not any bigger than Molly Gertrude's living room, but the roof was entirely made of glass and shaped as a dome. It gave a most spectacular view of the blue sky above and the puffy clouds that were gently flowing by. The water was crystal clear, and the place smelled fresh and inviting.

But, what was not so pleasant was the cold wind blowing from the air conditioner. Swimming pools were usually warm and comfortable, but not this pool, and it even caused Molly Gertrude to shiver. Then she remembered that Hazel had mentioned something about the air conditioner being out of order.

But who cared about a broken air conditioner when there was a dead body? Hazel Brick was lying right next to a lounge chair, face down on the tiles, and was dressed in a light blue bathrobe. Captain Coakes was standing nearby, together with Dr. Biddle. The captain looked up in relief when he saw Molly Gertrude, but Dr. Biddle did not seem too pleased.

"Miss Grey," Coakes cried out. "Another murder. This is terrible." It appeared he was on the verge of tears as he pointed to the limp body of Hazel Brick.

With the help of Dora, Molly knelt down and studied the body. It appeared Hazel too was strangled. When Molly pulled part of the bathrobe away she could clearly see the marks of strangulation on Hazel's neck. The one eye that was visible stared like a dead fish into empty space. She had not died a peaceful death.

"It's the same killer," Dr. Biddle said. "And she's not been dead for very long. Couldn't be more than an hour."

Molly Gertrude looked up. "How do you know, Doctor?"

He shrugged his shoulders. "Just feel her body. It's not stiff yet. What's more, the strangulation marks indicate the killer used the same method, although he used a different cloth this time. But the marks are almost identical to the marks on Mace Brick's neck. There's no doubt in my mind that this is the same murderer."

Molly Gertrude's mind worked fast and furious. Would a woman be strong enough to strangle a strong, husky body like that of Hazel Brick? She doubted it, but of course, a man could have done it together with a woman.

It was then that Molly Gertrude spotted a pair of flip-flops, standing right next to the pool chair. In a flash she recalled the strange encounter she just had with Guillermo DaCosta… an encounter without flip-flops.

"Whose are those?" Molly Gertrude asked Captain Coakes.

He shrugged his shoulders. "I suppose they are Hazel's," he said, apparently not thinking flip-flops were such a big deal.

"I doubt it," Molly Gertrude said as she shook her head. "Hazel Brick was *so* concerned about her looks… She would not likely wear something so ordinary." She thought for a moment and then asked, "Tell me, Captain, who all has access to this pool?"

"No one, really," he said. "Whoever wants to use this pool has to ask me for the key. I am the only one with the key."

"And why is that?"

"We like to keep this pool private so the guests can have total privacy. If every Tom, Dick and Harry can walk in at any time, it wouldn't be very private, would it? That's why we have a bigger pool on the lower deck."

Molly Gertrude sat down on one of the pool chairs and closed her eyes. Some things just didn't make sense… It was all in the details… Was she overlooking something…?

Then it came to her in a flash. She opened her eyes again, and looked up at Captain Coakes. "Captain," she said, "I think I may know what has happened."

"You do? What? Who?" Captain Coakes urged her to tell.

"Yes," Dr. Biddle added. "Please tell us."

"It's too early to tell," Molly Gertrude replied, "but if my hunch is right, we will soon find out. I would like to request a meeting together with several of the guests."

"Of course," Captain Coakes replied. "Which of the guests would you like to see?"

"I would like a meeting right away with Guillermo DaCosta, Cornelia Callmedt, her husband Harry, and Geoffrey Brick and his fiancée Evelyn." She turned to Dr. Biddle and said, "You don't mind coming too, do you Doctor?"

Biddle's face flushed. "Me? Why, I've got nothing to do with it."

"Still, I would like you to come," Molly Gertrude said. "It could prove to be very helpful."

Captain Coakes' face darkened. "I hope you know what you are doing, Miss Grey. Are these all suspects? These are respected guests."

"I know," Molly Gertrude replied, "but I urge you to do it nevertheless. And there's one other thing I would like you to do for me."

"Sure. What's that?"

Molly Gertrude leaned over to the Captain and motioned for him to come closer. When he did, she whispered something into his ear. At last he nodded.

"No problem, Miss Grey, I will do as you ask, although I do not understand why."

"Good," Molly Gertrude replied. "When do you think we can have the guests lined-up?"

"In half an hour, Miss Grey," Captain Coakes replied. "We'll meet in the library."

CHAPTER NINE

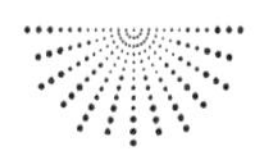

Half an hour later, on Captain Coakes' orders, First Mate Harrison had assembled the ones Molly Gertrude had asked to see, and they stood, huddled together, in front of the library on the far end of the upper deck.

"Why are we here?" Geoffrey Brick wanted to know, but Harrison shrugged his shoulders, gave the young man an apologetic smile and went to open the door. To his surprise it was locked. "Sorry," he said. "Captain has the key. He'll be here any second."

"What a waste of time," Cornelia murmured. "I don't even like libraries."

"Calm down, dear," her husband Harry said in a comforting voice. "I am sure it's all for the best."

Guillermo DaCosta, a pair of shiny, brown loafers on his feet, kept a bit to the side and did not seem comfortable at all. Geoffrey was holding Evelyn's hand, his face no longer a picture of gentleness, as his eyes had a worried, nervous stare.

At last, Captain Coakes, Molly Gertrude and Dora walked up.

"Thank you for coming," Captain Coakes told the waiting guests, "but why aren't you inside?"

"Door's locked," Harrison grunted.

Captain Coakes frowned. "How stupid of me," he said, "I asked the cleaning lady to do some deep-cleaning there this morning. She must have locked the place and forgotten to give me the key." He gave the guests a sheepish, frustrated grin, pulled out his phone, and pushed a few buttons.

"Dax," they heard him say, "can you come up for a minute. The door to the library is locked. I need you to unlock it."

"Sorry again," he sighed, "but these are trying days, and it appears a lot of things have gone wrong."

Luckily they didn't have long to wait, as almost immediately Dax appeared with his big set of keys and he quickly opened the door. It was a cozy place, a typical library, but not much bigger than the private swimming pool. The walls were lined with rows of books, and in the middle stood a round table with reading lamps and chairs.

"Is that all, Captain?" Dax asked. "I am busy fixing the Waste Heat Recovery Boiler, and as it turns out, it's a rather demanding job."

"Never mind the boiler for now," Captain Coakes said. "Just stay. I've got Harrison here, but your strength may come in handy. We are about to expose the murderer."

Dax nodded, and took position near the door. The others pulled out chairs from under the round table, and sat down.

"Miss Grey has explained to me what she thinks has happened," Captain Coakes began. "And what she says makes a lot of sense..." he paused for a moment, and then added, "... she believes that one of you here has killed both Mace and Hazel Brick."

"What?" A wave of horror rolled over the ones in the library.

"Ridiculous," Cornelia began to yell. "I hated Mace Brick, it's true... but I didn't kill him."

Her husband rubbed her back. "Calm down, sweetie pie, watch your blood pressure."

Molly Gertrude raised her hand and tried to bring order. "Please, be calm, and let me explain to you what I think happened."

The guests peered nervously at each other as if they were hoping to see who was capable of such horrendous crimes.

Molly Gertrude cleared her throat. "Geoffrey and Evelyn…" she said and she directed her attention to the couple, "You both have been on my list of suspects, but I don't think you did it. Neither of you seem capable of murder."

"As if *we* are," Cornelia Callmedt cried out upon hearing these words. "I thought murders get solved with proof, and not by feelings."

Molly Gertrude ignored Cornelia's outburst and continued. "Geoffrey, did you know that your father forced your wife-to-be, Evelyn, to sign a document that would pretty much give her no legal rights whatsoever, and would put both you and her at your father's mercy…" She waited to see the effect of her words on Geoffrey.

"W-What?" The blood drained from Geoffrey's face

and he turned to Evelyn. "Did my father force you into a legal agreement? Why did I not know about it?"

Evelyn burst out crying. "Because I love you, Geoffrey. Your father has been very mean to me, and told me all kinds of horrible things would happen to me, if I did not sign or ever told you about it."

Geoffrey jumped up, seething anger coursing through his body. "I'll destroy him... I'll get my dad for that," he burst out in anger. "I will..." He stopped halfway as he realized how ridiculous he sounded. His father was already dead.

Molly Gertrude continued. "This would have been a motive for killing him, but I don't think you knew about it." She turned to Evelyn. "And you, Evelyn? Could you have done such a wicked deed?" Evelyn was softly weeping, but Molly Gertrude shook her head. "I don't think you had the strength for it. I must be very mistaken if you are a killer."

"Feelings again," Cornelia yelled. "Where's the proof. Looks can be deceiving. I am going to put on a baby face too."

"Cornelia," her husband Harry said in alarm. "Don't say such things. Please, calm down."

"There is proof, Mrs. Callmedt," Molly Gertrude said. "They have an alibi for the night of the murder of Mr. Brick, and neither Geoffrey, nor Evelyn had access to the swimming pool."

"Well, I have an alibi too," Cornelia hissed.

Molly Gertrude turned her attention to Cornelia, "Mrs. Callmedt, it appears not many people know that you are actually Geoffrey's real mother. Are you?"

"I am," Cornelia said, "but what does that have to do with anything. I am not hiding anything. Mace told me not to ever mention it to anyone here on the ship. But since he's dead now, I suppose I can say whatever I want. Yes, I am Geoffrey Brick's mother."

Dr. Biddle let out a huff, and gave Cornelia an incredulous stare.

"You and your husband Harry do have a motive for killing Mace Brick," Molly Gertrude continued, "You have been greatly duped by the Bricks. They promised you financial assistance, but instead they virtually ruined you. That must not have made you very happy."

"It didn't," Cornelia replied. "I already told you I

hated Mace, but that doesn't mean I killed him. My husband and I have an alibi too."

"It's true," Molly Gertrude confirmed. "We talked to Amram Boletti, and he confirmed you both were in the recreation room all night, although his story is slightly different than yours. You *didn't* dance all night with your husband."

Cornelia blushed and looked down.

"What?" Harry Callmedt blurted it out. "What did you say, Cornelia?"

"Nothing," his wife looked at him with angry eyes. "Nothing of importance."

"I'll help out," Molly Gertrude offered. "On the night of Mace Brick's murder, you, Mr. Callmedt, were sleeping it off on a bench in the kitchen, so you could not have possibly murdered Mace Brick. And your wife couldn't have done it either, as she was indeed dancing all night, although not with you. She was dancing all night with Rasheed Biddle. Then, at three in the morning, long after the murder had already been committed, your wife and Rasheed left the recreation room together for places unknown."

Cornelia's husband's face turned pale and he jumped up as if he had been bitten by a snake. "Tell me this isn't true," he yelled at his wife. "You danced and walked off with Rasheed Biddle? Tell me Miss Grey is just making it up." He turned to Biddle and showed him his fists. "If I find out this is true, I'll get you for this, Biddle."

"Calm down, Harry," Cornelia growled. "Just be thankful you won't be charged with murder. This charade between us has been going on long enough and please spare me your bulldozer language. It's true, Rasheed and I have been seeing each other for some time now, but it's your own fault. You are just boring and never do anything. You never did and you never will."

"I-I…" Harry Callmedt stumbled over his words and then turned to Molly Gertrude. "Miss Grey," he said, "I want a divorce."

Molly Gertrude scratched her head. "Sorry, Mr. Callmedt, I am not a divorce attorney. I am a wedding planner that solves mysteries."

Dr. Biddle was shifting uneasily in his seat. "So… uh," he mumbled while he raised his hand in the air, as if he was sitting in first grade and asked permission to go to the bathroom. "I am off the hook too then I suppose," he said.

"It appears so," Molly Gertrude clucked her tongue.

"Although you sure were no friend of the Bricks either."

All eyes now turned to Guillermo DaCosta. He was the only one left.

"Murderer," Biddle croaked and cast the man an ugly look. "I thought you were a decent fellow."

"Not so fast, Doctor," Molly Gertrude spoke. "Let the man speak for himself."

Sweat formed on Guillermo's forehead, and his charm seemed long gone. Instead of the happy-go-lucky womanizer, he appeared more like a wounded bird trying to run away from a greedy tomcat. "I-I didn't murder Mace or Hazel. I know it looks like I did, but I didn't."

Molly Gertrude reached for a paper bag and pulled out the pair of flip-flops she had found next to the body of Hazel Brick. She studied Guillermo's desperate face. "Are these your thongs, Mr. DaCosta?"

For an instant, it appeared Guillermo would faint, but then he let out a deep grunt and nodded. "Yes, they are."

"They were found right next to the dead body of Mrs. Brick in the private swimming pool. You had no key to the pool and yet your flip-flops were there. Can you explain this to us?"

A hushed silence fell over the library. For a moment Guillermo did not speak, but then he sighed and said, "I-I had something going on with Hazel Brick. You know… something similar to what Dr. Biddle and Cornelia were having."

"What happened?" Molly Gertrude asked.

"We met in the private pool," Guillermo spoke slowly. "Hazel asked the Captain for the key and then let me in." He looked up while wringing his hands, "But please, Miss Grey, I didn't kill Hazel, nor Mace Brick."

"Just answer the question, Mr. DaCosta."

"On the night of Mace's murder, I was in the recreation room. You can ask Amram Boletti. I was busy—"

"—With the girls," Molly Gertrude answered the sentence. "I know, since we talked to Mr. Boletti. But I asked you about your flip-flops in the swimming pool…"

Guillermo sighed. "As I said, Hazel and I met in the pool this afternoon. We were going to have a bit of fellowship, but it was so cold there. The air conditioner was broken and I didn't like it at all."

"And then?"

"I told her it was too cold there, and I left. Hazel wanted to stay however, and asked me if she could use my flip-flops, since she was barefoot. I think she was afraid the vapors of the pool would ruin her high heeled shoes. She told me I should come back in an hour"

"Why?"

Guillermo shrugged his shoulders. "I think she wanted to get the air conditioner fixed."

"So you came back an hour later?"

"I did. The door to the pool was open, and when I peered inside, I saw Captain Coakes and Dr. Biddle standing over her dead body. I panicked and ran away. It's the honest truth. I didn't kill her. I loved her."

"So," Molly Gertrude said, "Then who committed those horrible crimes? Although you all seem to have a motive, you also all seem to have an alibi. What do we do now?"

For a moment an eerie silence hung over the place,

but then it was broken by a taunt from Dr. Biddle. "You just don't know, do you? I am out of here. What a farce this is."

"Wait, Dr. Biddle," Molly Gertrude replied. "I *do* know. The key to solving this mystery is the key."

The others stared at her in confusion.

"I'll explain," Molly Gertrude said. "Who has the key to both the Bricks' cabin and to the swimming pool? None of the guests have legal access to any of those doors. But there is somebody who does. There's one person, who has access to all the different places on the ship."

"Who?" Geoffrey cried out.

"The man with the master key," Molly Gertrude replied, and she turned her attention to First Engineer Dax.

Dax turned a shade of green.

"First Engineer Dax has such a key. He can open any door on this ship," Molly Gertrude stated.

"Ridiculous," Dax fumed. "Why would I be killing the Bricks? I didn't even know them before this journey."

Molly Gertrude raised her brows. "You didn't, Dax?

Or should I call you by your real name, Maxwell Dubois."

The others began to whisper excitedly in hushed tones.

"Yes," Molly Gertrude continued. "Our First Engineer is not really called Dax, but Dubois." She pulled the scrapbook she had found in Mace Brick's cabin out of the bag near her feet and opened it to the condemning article from Wilson Crook. She pointed to the photograph of Maxwell Dubois. "Does this picture look like our First Engineer?"

All eyes went forward. "I-It does," Geoffrey exclaimed, "except on the ship he's always wearing a beanie and sunglasses."

"Will you take off your glasses and your beanie, Dax?" Molly Gertrude demanded.

"I will not," Dax cried out, and all of a sudden, he made a run for the door.

"Harrison!" Captain Coakes cried out. "Grab the man."

Harrison was prepared. In one swift move he tackled the unfortunate engineer, took him in an iron grip, and stood him in front of Molly Gertrude and Captain Coakes.

"Well, Mr. Dax, what do you have to say for yourself?"

Dax cursed and stared at the floor for a moment, but at last he began to speak, his voice flat and without emotion. "It is as Miss Grey was saying. I was once a promising scientist. I worked at the same university as Mace Brick, but I found some glaring errors in his research in relation to Dark Matter. I published my findings, but the man went crazy." Dax shook his head in dismay. "In this world it seems money talks, and Mace had plenty of it. He knew who to bribe, and what lawyers to use. Even though he knew I was right, he ruined my career. He dragged me through the sewer and I was no longer wanted in the scientific community."

"So you were forced to take on another job," Molly Gertrude said.

Dax nodded. "I became an engineer. Then when I heard about this cruise to l'Ile du Fondu, I knew my time had come. I weaseled my way onto the ship and murdered Mace Brick. I was hoping to pin the blame on Hazel. I knew people would find out about her affair with Guillermo DaCosta, and that would not look good. That's why I used her shawl. I wasn't going to kill Hazel. I had nothing against her, but she called on me to fix the air conditioner in the swimming pool..."

"And then, when you entered the pool, she recognized you?" Molly Gertrude said.

"She did," Dax replied. "I had not expected Hazel to be inside the pool, and thus I wasn't wearing my sunglasses. But the moment I came in she recognized me, and knew it was I that had killed her husband."

"And then?"

Dax shrugged his shoulders. "She started to scream and... well you can fill in the details. I am not proud of what I've done."

"Lock him up," Captain Coakes ordered Harrison.

Harrison nodded. "Where, Captain?"

Captain Harrison thought for a moment and then turned to Molly Gertrude and Dora. "How much time do you need to clear out your cabin, Miss Grey?"

"One minute at the most," Dora replied before Molly Gertrude could answer.

Captain Coakes pressed his lips together and said, "Good. We will lock the scoundrel up in Miss Grey's cabin, until we can hand him over to the police. And you Miss Grey and Miss Brightside, can stay for now in the King's suite on the upper deck." He hesitated. "If you'd like of course. It's the best place on board this ship, but I think you both deserve it."

Molly Gertrude hesitated, but again, Dora answered for them both. "That would be lovely, Captain. We would be honored with such a wonderful gesture."

EPILOGUE

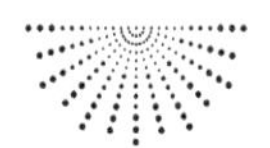

Dora and Molly Gertrude got to enjoy the King's suite for only three days. In counsel with Geoffrey and Evelyn it was decided they would turn the ship around immediately and go back to Oyster Bay Port. Even though the killer was locked up in Molly Gertrude and Dora's old cabin, nobody was in a party mood anymore, and everyone wanted to get back home and have the killer safely handed over to the authorities.

When they arrived at Oyster Bay Port in the late afternoon, Geoffrey handed Molly Gertrude a generous check for her hard work.

"I am a rich man now," he told Molly Gertrude. "I inherited all my dad's wealth. But if it had not been for the two of you, my future may have looked a lot bleaker. Thank you from the bottom of my heart."

"You still need a wedding planner?" Molly Gertrude asked. She grinned and added, "We'll give you a discount."

Geoffrey smiled, but shook his head. "No, Miss Grey. Evelyn and I will marry quietly, in a little country church. No frills, no extravaganza... Nothing. Just her and me, the pastor, and the rings." Then he bent forward and placed a gentle kiss on Molly Gertrude's cheek. "You remind me of my grandmother. She was a real saint. I will never forget you, Miss Grey. Thank you again."

Then he turned around and walked off.

In the distance Molly Gertrude could hear the sound of the train station. She swallowed hard. They still had quite a long trip back to Calmhaven.

"Come on Dora," she said. "The train is waiting."

"Still bored, Miss Molly Gertrude? Dora asked with a grin, as they walked off the gangplank.

Molly Gertrude shook her head. "No, Dora. No longer bored. I really, really want to go home. I miss my cat Misty, my house... I miss Calmhaven."

"And I miss Digby," Dora added.

Molly Gertrude frowned. "It didn't work out with, what's his name… Hamper Bosenlist?

"Hampus Rosenqvist," Dora corrected Molly Gertrude. "No, it didn't work out. He used way too much garlic in his dishes, even ate it raw, claiming it was good for his health. Thus his breath basically… well it stank. I can't wait until I see Digby again."

They both laughed as they exited the El Vivo and boarded the train back to Calmhaven. After all, there's no place like home.

Thank you so much for reading. We hope you really enjoyed the story. Please consider leaving a positive review on Amazon if you did.

LOOKING FOR MORE OF MOLLY?

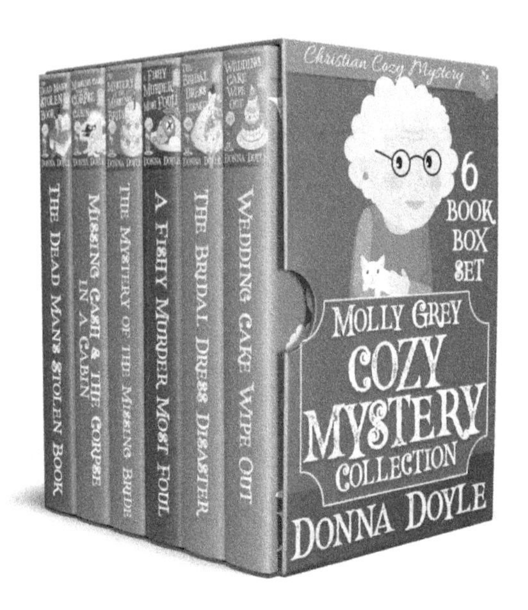

Join Molly, Dora and the array of quirky Calmhaven characters for 6 full blown cozy mysteries in the *Molly Grey Cozy Mystery Collection*.

Click here to start reading right now - free on Kindle Unlimited!

CPSIA information can be obtained
at www.ICGtesting.com
Printed in the USA
LVHW011038291019
635547LV00001B/122/P